Death Steals A Kiss

A Taylor Texas Mystery

VIKKI WALTON

Morewellson, Ltd.

Death Steals A Kiss

Cover design by The Cover Vault

Formatting by Rik – Wild Seas Formatting

CHAPTER ONE

Christie fought the urge to flee as six pairs of eyes all turned to fix their gaze on her.

"Fine, I'll do it. But this is the first and last time I'm going to be the mc for any fundraiser."

Smiles broke forth on faces and heads nodded in unison.

"Great." Lana replied. "Now, let's go to the next item on the agenda. That would be catering."

Christie barely heard the conversation as the sounds of loud clanging came through the office door. A door to the interior room burst open, and one of the volunteers of the equine rescue came rushing inside.

"There's been an accident. Gabe's been hurt."

Seats were shoved back as everyone rushed outside to see a man lying on the ground. Others surrounded him while the electrical contractor's supervisor spoke on the phone.

"Is that nine-one-one?" Christie blurted out as the man nodded. She rushed to the injured man, kneeling down next to him. "Help's on the way, Gabe. Don't move."

While it had been over six years since Christie had hung up her nursing career, she still knew that Gabe's vitals were critical. She did the only thing she could do until the medical teams arrived; she held his left hand and prayed he wasn't suffering.

Shushed voices and a few sobs came from those standing by helplessly. A hand touched her shoulder. It was the supervisor. He bent down and spoke softly, "They're on their way." He glanced at Gabe and as his eyes met Christie's, a look of sadness passed between them. It was clear they both knew that the prospects for Gabe didn't bode well.

It seemed like forever before they heard the sirens of a firetruck and an ambulance approaching. The medical tech jumped from the firetruck, carrying a large bag with him. They were asked to step back, and Christie noted that many of the board members were huddled together, whispering among themselves.

As she moved back, her foot hit a piece of metal. The ladder. Christie turned and studied the position of the ladder and pieces of the scaffolding scattered across the floor. From the looks of it, Gabe must have been up on one of the tall ladders and it had fallen, taking him with it. In an effort to stop the fall, he must have reached out for the scaffolding but, unfortunately, it had come away as well., taking him with it.

Landing on a concrete floor, she noticed he wasn't wearing his hardhat. Maybe he was just going up to retrieve something. No, that was one thing she'd liked about hiring this group. They were strict on safety for their employees and anyone that went around the work they were doing. When they'd begun, they'd even had a safety talk for the staff and the volunteers. That's when she'd first met Gabe, who had been overseeing the work for them to hang more lighting for the upcoming gala.

She glanced toward the ceiling where he'd

been working. There was a series of scaffolding in place as the electrical contracting company worked on the lighting. If he'd been using the ladder to access the upper lofts and then crossed over to the main scaffold to get back to it, had he stumbled on the way down? Off in the corner, she saw a hardhat with the company name, Bryson, on it. It must have come off when he fell.

As the medical team worked on Gabe, one of the board members pointed out a new arrival at the front door. Christie spied a woman who must be the writer she'd agreed to give an interview to for the local paper, *The Comfort Bulletin*.

Oh no. This was terrible timing, but better to get it over with, as there was nothing she could do to help Gabe and she didn't want to reschedule. It had been difficult making this time free with all the last minute gala items on top of regular operations.

The woman, who looked to be in her thirties, pushed her designer sunglasses up on her head, revealing the auburn roots in her golden blonde hair. "What's going on?"

"An accident. The electrician putting up some extra lighting for the gala." Christie stood directly in front of the woman to block her vision. The one thing that Christie knew intimately, having worked decades as a hospice nurse, were the signs of impending death. Gabe deserved better than people gawking over him as he took his last breaths. And she'd seen miracles happen when people survived. Either way, it was no business of the woman standing in front of her.

"Everyone, please. Let's give them some room." Christie's eyes met Lana's, who nodded and began escorting board members and volunteers back into the office space and away from the barn area. Once they had made their way back up to the main offices inside the administration section of the barn, Christie motioned to the woman. "I'm sorry, um, Teresa, right? Let's go upstairs to my office." Christie motioned for the young woman to follow her through to her office.

Christie strode inside and made her way around her desk, overflowing with papers and other office paraphernalia. Even though she tried to use the computer for most things, Christie had finally given up, as her mind didn't work that way. She looked up at the whiteboard facing her desk, post-it's in an assortment of colors showing at a glance what was upcoming, in process or done. With the gala taking so much time, there were few colors in the area for the items that were done. Christie's top priority was to remedy that soon. But this thing with Gabe meant that her mind and most of the others would be on him today. Christie sat in her swivel office chair while she motioned for Teresa to take a seat opposite her in one of the upholstered chairs. The chairs had been Bob's, one of the board members, taken from his offices when he'd retired. He'd also donated his large mahogany desk, but it simply wouldn't work. In the end, they'd convinced him to sell his desk and chair and give the money to Horse Haven. Christie had been shocked when he came by with a check for fifteen thousand dollars. She couldn't imagine spending that much money on a desk and chair. Turned out that had only been for

the desk as the buyer didn't want the chair which had seen lots of use over the years. Christie had been the recipient and now sat in the large leather chair. She clasped her hands on her desk, took in a deep breath, and readied herself for the interview.

"Thanks for meeting with me. I'm sorry it comes as such a horrible time. Was there an accident?"

"Yes, Gabe—" Christie stopped herself from saying *was a nice guy.* She needed to stay focused. He was well cared for with the medical crew. Miracles happened. She shot up another quick prayer for him and those working on him. Then turned her focus back on Teresa and the interview.

Focusing on what's in front of her had been one of the first things Christie had learned when she had gone into nursing. The ability to compartmentalize allowed you to retain your emotional stability and sanity. It's why she'd been able to work with dying patients day after day and not collapse in tears. She'd laughed with many of

them as they joked about things and sat with them as they cried over things they wished they wouldn't have put off in their life.

Christie placed her folded hands on the wooden desk. "Now, what would you like to know?"

"I have much of the basic information, but if you could give me a quick overview, just to make sure I have my facts correct?"

Christie nodded. "Sure."

Teresa set her phone down on the desk, "Okay if I record this? Sometimes my notes turn into scribbles even I can't read. It helps in case I can't recall something or need to add another piece of information to the article." She smiled at Christie. "Oh, before I forget, could I also get some pictures to include?"

"Sure. I can have Alice send you some. How many would you like?"

"If we could have one of the exterior, one of the horses, maybe one of the staff or volunteers, and any others you think might be appropriate."

"I'll have her send you some and also include

some of the program participants if they're okay with having their pictures used."

"Great. Those pictures help to draw people in to read the story. Also, I believe you're hosting your first gala?"

"Yes. It's our first big donor push."

"I'd be happy to include information on where to donate in the article if you'd like that."

"That would be great." Christie nodded. "Now, are we ready to begin?"

"Yes. How about a quick background on how you came to be on this place?"

"Okay, so let's see. My Pop owns part of this land, as does Curtis Altgelt. Oh, do you need full names?"

"I have those, so no worries. Plus, if I need anything else, I'll call you."

"Great. Some years back, Lana—the vet here—had an idea for an equine rescue. It was her dream, and we connected with other groups and looked into what they were doing." Christie stopped as the intercom sounded, asking about accepting a call. She rejected it and asked for all

calls to be held.

Christie sighed. "Wow, six years. Time sure flies, doesn't it? Lana went to vet school and during that time we started looking into helping horses that were either abandoned, their owners couldn't care for them any longer, or ill. We collaborate with vets in the Kendall county area for horses that need further rehabilitation and care that require oversight of their cases. We also board horses, so that helps pay for the services we provide and soon people wanted to donate to it. We filed our five-o-one-c-three to gain nonprofit status and this year we'll host our first major donor event."

Christie paused, but Teresa nodded for her to continue.

"That's what all the work is, that's going on now. We set up the first barn, and that's where the vets and techs office and most of the elderly or infirm horses are housed. We did a capital campaign, and this barn is the second phase. We'll use this as an event space and upstairs we have some small loft offices we lease out, which helps

pay overhead. In fact, that's how we acquired a couple of our board members." Christie paused, not sure how much background the woman wanted or required for her article, but when she still didn't respond with a question, Christie pressed on. "We had plenty of land for horses, so it was decided to build this place on the edge of both properties, with both my Pop and Curtis gifting the nonprofit with the land."

"So that equates to what, one hundred acres in total?"

"Approximately."

"That's a lot of land." Teresa scribbled something on her notepad.

"Not really. Horses need a lot of land, and we knew that this series of barns and other facilities would also require enough land. With parking and especially parking for horse trailers, it's not that much."

"Wasn't there some interest in buying this property? A lot of money was forfeited by gifting the land instead of selling it."

"They   wanted   to   build   a   housing

11

development. This ensures that most of the land will remain as its always been while providing care for aging or neglected horses." Christie stood and walked over to the window. "Sorry, want to see what's going on." She also wanted to stop this train of conversation. She spied the medical team still hovering around Gabe.

"I certainly understand. Does this accident mean that you'll still host the fundraiser?"

"I would think so. It's not for another month, anyway. We decided to have it in February on Saturday, the twelfth."

"Let's see here, the theme is Boots and Ballgowns, is that correct?" Teresa folded back her page, reading her notes.

"Yes. That's correct. The gala will be in the evening. During the morning, we're going to have some hayrides and pony rides, along with a petting farm for families. That night, we'll host the event for our donors and sponsors."

"Is that the way you support the nonprofit?"

"Actually, we do a combination of items. Donations, campaigns, and fee-for-service."

"Is that nine-one-one?" Christie blurted out as the man nodded. She rushed to the injured man, kneeling down next to him. "Help's on the way, Gabe. Don't move."

While it had been over six years since Christie had hung up her nursing career, she still knew that Gabe's vitals were critical. She did the only thing she could do until the medical teams arrived; she held his left hand and prayed he wasn't suffering.

Shushed voices and a few sobs came from those standing by helplessly. A hand touched her shoulder. It was the supervisor. He bent down and spoke softly, "They're on their way." He glanced at Gabe and as his eyes met Christie's, a look of sadness passed between them. It was clear they both knew that the prospects for Gabe didn't bode well.

It seemed like forever before they heard the sirens of a firetruck and an ambulance approaching. The medical tech jumped from the firetruck, carrying a large bag with him. They were asked to step back, and Christie noted that

CHAPTER ONE

Christie fought the urge to flee as six pairs of eyes all turned to fix their gaze on her.

"Fine, I'll do it. But this is the first and last time I'm going to be the mc for any fundraiser."

Smiles broke forth on faces and heads nodded in unison.

"Great." Lana replied. "Now, let's go to the next item on the agenda. That would be catering."

Christie barely heard the conversation as the sounds of loud clanging came through the office door. A door to the interior room burst open, and one of the volunteers of the equine rescue came rushing inside.

"There's been an accident. Gabe's been hurt."

Seats were shoved back as everyone rushed outside to see a man lying on the ground. Others surrounded him while the electrical contractor's supervisor spoke on the phone.

interview is over."

Christie pushed a button on her phone, "Alice, can you escort Teresa out please?"

"Well, goodbye then." Teresa picked up her phone, ending the recording.

"Goodbye." Christie waited until the woman had left before she sat, slumping in her chair. Oh geez. She certainly didn't want any issues to stop people from donating to the nonprofit if Teresa decided to do a hit piece versus a regular story. She better speak to Lana about the interview sooner than later.

Christie rose from her chair and watched as Teresa walked toward the door, but then quickly twisted back around as noise from below rose to the office. She rushed over to the front window overlooking the parking area. Another vehicle had joined the others. This one was a familiar sight.

The coroner had arrived.

CHAPTER TWO

After they had removed Gabe, the coroner came upstairs to let Christie know that they were done. She shook the man's hand and accepted his business card should she have any other questions. Christie returned to her chair, her eyes landing on the whiteboard that covered most of the wall across from her desk. She needed to get back to work as she couldn't stop moving forward with her responsibilities that needed to be accomplished.

Being tasked with the oversight of the nonprofit, day-to-day activities and now the gala, the creation of her ninety-day strategy focused on three primary areas. Post-it's in bright colors in the To Do space beckoned. She picked up a marker and added Gabe's family to the priority list. That poor family. He had gone to work, never knowing he would kiss his wife goodbye for the last time, or hug his kids, or so many other things that would now be left undone. Sadness spilled out of her heart and Christie allowed the tears to come for the man who died too young and the family that would be forever changed because of it. After composing herself, she blew her nose and wiped her hands with an antibacterial wipe.

She stood and placed the Post-it on the board glancing to the items in the In Progress area. Finalizing the table chart could be something she could look over with Alice to try and move it into the completed section. Though she figured table counts and attendees would be changing almost up to the date of the gala.

She noted those that had been moved to the bottom of the whiteboard. At least the ones in the Completed area were growing. Having this board where she could see everything at a glance had helped her to stay on top of things and not have things fall through the cracks.

On the top of the board, was a simple statement which read "Small things can impact other things which in turn lead to big things."

Gabe's death was a big thing. Would there be

fall-out on the nonprofit because of it? Or would it affect donors or volunteers? It was too early to tell. While his death was a tragic accident, that didn't mean it wouldn't nest in people's minds and make them leery about their support of the organization. Christie laid her head down on the desk as fatigue replaced the earlier rush of adrenaline. She doubted she'd get much else done today so best to go around and speak to people individually and allay any fears or worries. She pulled her jacket from the coat hook and fortified herself to confront the tragedy head on.

Hours later when the nonprofit closed down for the day, Christie was happy to release the tension she'd been holding as she made her way home.

Christie arrived home emotionally exhausted to find Pop snoozing by the crackling fire of her woodstove. Ever since her home construction had been finished and with her work at the nonprofit, they'd spent less time together. Part of the reason for Christie moving home was to spend more time with Pop. She didn't want to have regrets that she hadn't been available for the important things in life. Pop was all she had, though she loved Curtis, Lana, and her kids like they were her own family. Gabe's death had brought the reality of losing a loved one to the forefront of her mind. It was easy to forget the important things of life when you were busy pursuing other things that would one day fade away.

Because she'd gotten so busy with working at the nonprofit, Christie had suggested they make a weekly date to have dinners together on Thursdays. This allowed Pop to go to the Wednesday dinner at church and for them to eat lunch on Sunday with the others.

Christie's heart swelled whenever she thought back to how they'd all become a big extended family over the last years. While she'd enjoyed living an independent life, the closeness of family and friends were like a comfortable, old sweater you wore. It may have its flaws, but it kept you feeling warm and happy. Christie cherished the bond they shared more than anything.

Once the coroner had arrived and statements

were taken, Christie had called Pop to let him know an accident had happened and that she'd tell him more later. She also informed him that she might be late getting home. She'd advised him to go ahead and eat without her. But Pop wouldn't hear of it and said he'd handle the cooking, so she'd have a hearty meal ready whenever she got home.

Christie laid her hand on Pop's shoulder. He blinked as he jolted from his nap and glanced up at Christie. "Just resting my eyes for a bit 'till you got home."

"Thanks for starting a fire. It's nice to come home to that when there's a chill in the air. Also, something smells fantastic."

"Pot roast with roasted potatoes and carrots. It should be ready soon. Since you said you weren't sure when you'd be home, I started it a bit later."

Christie bent down and placed a kiss on her father's graying head. "Pop, I appreciate all you do, but I'm not keen on you climbing those stairs up to my place. You'll be seventy-six this spring."

Pop shook his head. "Where does the time go?"

When Christie had designed her cob house, she'd decided to raise it up on stilts so as to create a lower screened-in area. This held a long table, chairs and could be used for dinner or games. At the time, she liked the idea of being able to see views in every direction, and the sunrises and sunsets were marvelous from that height. However, she hadn't expected that Pop would ignore her pleas not to take the stairs without her around. Oh well, live and learn.

She sighed. "It definitely seems to go by faster than it used to—at least it seems that way for me. Still, it would be better if I were around in case you fell."

He rose from the chair. "I ain't dead yet. Stairs don't bother me none."

"Okay, well, let me change out of these work clothes and then we can—"

Pop interrupted Christie. "Curtis called me with some disturbing news today. Is it right?"

"News travels fast round here. Yes, Gabe fell

from a ladder is what we think. He must have hit his head on the concrete, would be my guess."

"Well, ain't that a shame. Gabe and Maria are good people. Poor kids."

Christie nodded while she shucked out of her jacket. She slung it over her arm as she headed into the bedroom, where she hung it up before pulling off her maroon cowgirl boots. Stripping off her jeans and hunter green, long-sleeved polo shirt embroidered with the Horse Haven logo, she pulled on a warm blue fleece top with a pair of yoga pants. She left on her socks, which were decorated with pie slices, a gift from Lana and the kids at Christmas. Had it only been a few weeks ago? Gabe's death was a horrible way to start the new year. She went over and made a note to see about putting together a basket for Gabe's family from the nonprofit.

Padding out to the living area, she saw Pop over at the woodstove, holding the top of a cast iron Dutch-oven that was on the stove's burner up top.

"Pop, I'll make the gravy if you can grab the

plates and silverware." Christie took the pot over to the kitchen stove, where she removed the meat and vegetables onto a large serving dish she placed on the granite countertop.

"What about biscuits?"

"Sure nuff. Sounds mighty good."

Christie used self-rising flour and a cup of heavy cream to make the biscuits. As she slid the pan into the oven, she set to work using the pan drippings and whisking milk and flour together. As soon as the brown gravy was ready, they sat down at the table.

After they'd prayed for Gabe's family, they ate in silence. Finally, Pop spoke. "I had a call from a reporter today. She wanted to know about—"

"Oh no. Was it Teresa?"

He nodded. "Seemed pretty nosy."

"Unfortunately, I think she's trying to make her article more juicy than factual. She was there when the accident happened. So much for publicity for the rescue."

"I wouldn't pay her no, never mind. How's the board coming along?"

Christie thought back to the morning's events. They'd finally put together a good group of community members for the board. There was Bob Wilkins, who owned a truck dealership now after his retirement from the bank and had been voted in as treasurer. Amy Rogers, who owned a farm and feed store, had been elected secretary. While Lana was the founder of the nonprofit, she had chosen to serve on the board as a co-chair along with Don Miller, an insurance broker, as the other co-chair. This way she could bow out in case there were issues that might cause conflict as far as vet salary or benefits. Two other members made up the current board. Becky Anderson owned horses and also raised alpacas on her place while Carol Swift, a homeschooling mom of five, had a disabled child and had gotten engaged with the nonprofit after becoming interested in the equine therapy the nonprofit provided. Curtis and Pop served in an advisory capacity for anything that pertained to the land where the rescue was located.

"Hello?" Pop's words brought her back.

"Sorry, Pop. Just thinking about the board. I think we've got a good mix and while we'd like a few more people, this should work for now. With some of the other board members moving or not serving a second term, we should be good for the next three to five years."

He set his fork down. "What about you? Planning on staying on as director?"

Christie shook her head. "No. I'm not sure what I want to do yet. I don't see this as something I'll do long-term."

"Well, one day at a time." He patted her hand.

After they'd washed up the dishes, Christie watched as Pop took the stairs down to where his truck waited. She should add some lighting to illuminate the steps. That could be helpful for going up and down at night, for her as well as Pop. She waved as Pop drove back to his house. She went inside and put on another log, sparks flying and wood popping. She settled into a large, deeply cushioned chair next to the woodstove, her mind replaying the scene of this morning.

Everyone had rushed out to where Gabe lay

on the floor. Wait, that didn't seem right. Bob had been in front of her with Amy and Carol, closely followed by Lana. It had been a pretty long meeting, and everyone had excused themselves at some point to visit the bathroom facilities and take some breaks from the meeting to grab more coffee or breakfast burritos.

But that wouldn't have impacted Gabe's fall unless someone had done something to the scaffolding or the ladder. But why would someone do something to Gabe? He was a great guy. Tears pooled in Christie's eyes. He had his whole life ahead of him. For it to be snuffed out so quickly and tragically wasn't fair. But who said life was fair? Look at what Lana had dealt with, losing her husband in the war, and some of the other things over the few years since she'd moved to Texas.

Christie's mind kept going back to the morning of the accident. She wanted to make sure that she did her due diligence as the nonprofit could be held responsible. She needed to talk to Dave about their policy. Everyone was accounted for when the accident happened, but had they all been inside the office at that time? Christie struggled to remember. Christie gazed into the flames in the woodstove's window, willing herself to remember where everyone stood before the medical personnel showed up. She sighed. It didn't matter. It was a tragic accident, plain and simple. She pulled a fluffy cream throw around her waist and reached for the book she'd been reading on nonprofit best practices when her phone trilled.

"Hello?"

It was Don Miller. "Christie, sorry to call so late, but after today, I couldn't get it out of my mind."

"No worries. I had made a note to call you tomorrow, so great minds and all that. Why are you calling, Don?"

"I've gone back over the nonprofit's policies, and I'm concerned we could be sued for Gabe's death. I think we may need to consider our amount of insurance and even obtain an umbrella policy. We should be all right, but if something else were to happen, well, it could shut the nonprofit down. I think we should call an emergency meeting to discuss it."

"That's scary to even think about. If you think so. But that's not my decision. That would be up to you and Lana."

"Oh, yeah, right. I'll give Lana a call." He hung up.

"Well, goodbye to you too." Christie spoke aloud. As far as she knew, the nonprofit was insured by another agency, so it wouldn't be a conflict of interest for Don to advise that they look into more insurance. Thankfully, she only had to worry about the minimal staff, which comprised an administrative assistant, a volunteer coordinator, a bookkeeper, and a facilities maintenance guy. Lana oversaw all the vet techs and that end of the operation. She would help them through the fundraiser, but after that she wanted to get serious about her role there. If she did decide to quit her position, she wanted to ensure that they had plenty of time to look for a new executive director.

She picked up the book but after reading the

same paragraph three times in a row, gave up. Her brain wasn't going to deal with any more work today. She should call Teresa tomorrow and ensure that she stayed on track with her article about the rescue. They needed that article to focus on the work being done for the horses and the riders receiving therapy, not turn in a salacious gossip piece. She also needed to talk to Tom, the facilities guy, to see how they could ensure better safety measures for in the future. She played through the events again and as she did, she realized that four people had left the office during their meeting not long before Gabe fell. Could they have done something to the ladder Gabe was using and if so, what would be their motive?

"Will you stop it!" Christie admonished herself. She knew that tragic accidents occurred. But that's not what kept popping into her mind. It was more the fear of what chain of events had been initiated because of it.

That's what had Christie worried.

CHAPTER THREE

The sun's rays peeked in through her window as Christie woke the next morning. She stretched and enjoyed the pause between waking up and getting started on her day. Thankfully, it was Saturday, so she didn't have to go in to work. It would also allow for everyone to settle in with their thoughts after the accident. She padded into the kitchen, hitting the button on the coffeemaker that she'd set up the night before. The smell of roasted coffee beans filled the air with their fragrant aroma. After the coffeemaker beeped, Christie pulled on a pair of slides and a long jacket before taking the coffee outside on the screened-in deck that comprised part of the north-eastern side of the house.

Even though the morning's air was chilly with the humidity, the sun's warmth enveloped her as she pressed both hands around the steaming cup. She sighed with contentment as her gaze went over the scenery which was now laden with frost. A tree close to the house, dripped with water, letting her know that the picturesque beauty she now beheld would be temporary. She settled into one of two wooden rockers, with padded back and seats in a barn-red buffalo check pattern.

Christie blew on the coffee before taking a sip of the hot brew, allowing its warmth to travel through her. Shielding her eyes with her hand, she spied some Axis deer grazing off in the distance. She picked up the binoculars on the table next to her and swiveled in her seat to see a large dually pickup arriving at the nonprofit.

Lana opened the door and climbed out, wearing a chambray jacket and her hair pulled back in a high ponytail. Last week, they'd had an aging mare come in and Lana was watching over the old lady with great care. In some ways, Christie realized that Lana was no less a hospice nurse than she had been. She was also thankful for Tom, who had a small apartment on-site in the building. They also had cameras that looked over the paddocks and interior bays, so at night he could keep watch.

Christie sat up. The cameras. Why h̲
thought of that? It would at least giv̲   ̲ ̲e
closure to how Gabe's accident had occurred. She
set the binoculars down and went inside to get
dressed. Shucking into her jeans, a t-shirt, and
topping that with a flannel shirt, she rolled up the
sleeves of the blue shirt. Pulling on her boots, she
grabbed a cap from the coat rack to corral her
unruly curls.

Grabbing a left-over biscuit from last night,
she smeared it with peanut butter and local
honey, before taking a delicious bite, crumbs
dusting her shirt which she brushed into the sink.
Taking one last swallow of the now tepid coffee,
Christie grabbed her work jacket from the peg
next to the door.

Deciding to get in a ride, Christie made her
way down to the barn, where she saddled up
Champ before heading to *Horse Haven*. As she
made her way toward the rescue, she enjoyed the
morning ride as the sun grew warm on her back.
Taking Champ over would allow her to lead one of

the other horses for some exercise, as she didn't have much she needed to accomplish at home.

She dismounted, waving at Rory, a faithful volunteer who met her at the barn doors, hauling a wheelbarrow full of hay.

"Morning, Rory All good?"

He nodded. "Uh, huh." Rory wasn't much of a talker, but he was a hard worker.

"Great. Listen, I thought I might take Chester out for a walk with Champ. Would that be okay?'

"Yep." He lifted the wheelbarrow and walked off toward the paddock.

Christie grinned. Wow, three whole words. "Okay. Later then."

She made her way inside, waving at Lana before heading upstairs to the offices. She passed down the hall and past the bathrooms to where an office had been set aside for the cameras and monitors, along with other maintenance and security items. Christie sat down in the swivel chair and pulled up the recording from yesterday on the monitor. She pressed play and scrolled quickly through the earlier time until she came to the moment where Gabe fell.

Wait, something wasn't right. She went back to when the board members started arriving. She watched as everyone entered, chatting with one another as they made their way up to the offices. There was footage of Lana speaking with Tom, as well as other volunteers who came and went. She stopped the footage when she saw Gabe enter the barn. He was carrying his hardhat under his left arm, and a lunchbox in the other. Tears glistened as she knew how lovingly Maria always prepared Gabe's lunches for him. He went out of sight and the next thing on the screen was when people were running toward him.

No, that can't be right. She reversed the footage and replayed it again, this time looking at the timestamp. Someone had either stopped the tape during that time and then re-started it or had erased the footage. But who would do that? More importantly, why would they do it? If Gabe's death had been an accident, it made no sense.

Christie sat back in her chair, her fingers steepled in contemplation. She needed to talk to

Lana about it. There had been something on that tape someone didn't want others to see. Whoever had fixed the tape had also done a good job of making it appear that nothing was amiss. If you'd been glancing at it, chances are that the deleted minutes wouldn't even be registered in the viewer's mind.

Since the room was left open during the day, anyone could have access to the computers or office supplies. She saved the recording in the cloud and then made her way out of the room, locking it behind her. She'd need to let others know that from now on, the door needed to remain locked during working hours and at night. She'd leave a note for Alice, her administrative assistant, that anyone needing access would have to come through her to unlock the door.

Now that she had this knowledge, what should she do with it? Was this something for the Sheriff, the coroner, or someone else? Lana would be busy all morning, so she'd have to wait to get her opinion on it. For now, she could take out the horses for some exercise.

She made her way downstairs and to the back of the barn to head outside. Next door she found Rory filling the horse's feed into their stalls. "I'm ready for Chester."

Rory coaxed the old boy from out of his stall. The old gelding rarely wanted to venture outside, but once he and Champ had bonded, he was okay following him for walks on the property. She'd returned Chester back to Rory when she saw Lana sitting outside, taking a break. Now would be a good time to talk with her.

"Lana, I have something I want to share with you."

The woman shielded her eyes. "Me first. Okay?"

"Okay." Christie took a seat next to her.

"I got a call from Teresa—"

"Oh, no. Please tell me she isn't opening old wounds."

"She's trying, but I think I can handle her. I, well, I may have hinted that we may have a couple of spots at the Gala depending on when the article comes out."

Christie removed her jacket and sat down next to Lana. "Why you little minx. I wish I would have thought of that."

"But now I feel bad. It's pretty much a bribe to print good things."

"More like you aren't going to take any guff from someone who's trying to stir up trouble. I think you did the right thing." Christie draped the coat over her arms.

Lana faced Christie. "You do? I hardly slept last night thinking about it."

Christie crossed her legs. "I wouldn't give it another thought. However, there is something that we do need to discuss."

"Yes?"

"Someone doctored the video footage before Gabe's accident."

"What?" Lana replied.

"Deleted or did something to the footage. There's a gap. It's not long, but it's definitely there. I want us to lock the door to the office supply room during the day from now on. I plan to let the volunteers know that Alice will need to open the door for them."

"Okay, good. But does this mean—" Lana's eyes grew wide.

"That Gabe was murdered? I don't know, but someone had to have a reason for deleting that footage. We need to figure out why. And more importantly, who." Christie rose from her seat. "I also need to figure out if I should share this information with someone."

"I think you should call the coroner. He may be interested in hearing that news, since I believe he's the one who'll be investigating."

Christie nodded. "Yes, that's what I've been thinking, but wasn't sure. I'll call him tomorrow."

"Tomorrow's Sunday." Lana smiled.

"Oh yeah. My days seem to run into one another." Christie replied.

Lana stood up. "Well, I need to get back to it. See you tomorrow after church for lunch?"

Christie nodded, "Of course. You know Pop."

"Great." Lana started into the barn before turning back to Christie. "Oh, I forgot. The caterer is bringing in food on Monday so we can do some taste-testing."

"It's a bit early for that, isn't it? The gala's still a month away."

"Yes, but she wanted to do it since we didn't do anything over the holidays. Plus, who doesn't like a free lunch for the staff and volunteers?"

"True. Do I need to do anything? Set up a space?"

Lana replied, "No. She was here yesterday, so she picked out the best spot for the catering area."

"Okay. Good." Christie waved before heading back to mount Champ and ride home. As she made her way past Mesquite trees, it occurred to Christie that the caterer had also been present yesterday. The first thing Christie needed to do when she got home was make a list of everyone who had been on the premises of *Horse Haven* and could have seen what happened to Gabe.

Or worse, could have had a hand in his death.

CHAPTER FOUR

After church on Sunday, Christie made her way over to Lana's. It seemed so funny thinking of Curtis's old house as Lana's now, but it felt like the old homestead had taken on a new life with Lana and the kids in the big house.

Curtis had moved into a tiny home on the property with a deck built off the back for him and his cronies to sit and chat or play dominoes. Christie pulled up outside the house and alighted to see the kids sitting outside with friends.

One thing that Christie admired was the way Lana ensured her kids were well-rounded and spent a lot of time away from computer or television screens. They'd grown up with daily chores which may have been a hold-over from the military life Lana used to live. Plus, not having much access to online pursuits had enabled them to delve deep into talents and skills that had been buried.

Lana's daughter, Allie, was much like her mother in caring for animals and had taken to gardening too. On the weekends, she'd often find Allie working alongside the volunteers in creating plantings around the barns of native flowers and Xeriscape perennials.

Christie couldn't wait to see the fields in the spring covered in blue bonnets and cheerful paintbrush flowers. Carol, one of the board members, had suggested that it would make beautiful places for photography and people could donate to use the landscape as a backdrop. The board had all agreed, and Carol was thrilled when the board stated that any of those donations would be designated for the equine therapy program. Carol's daughter was a participant, and she'd been instrumental in getting the word out about the program. Plus, she'd gotten Lana excited about expanding the program for veterans and their families.

Christie waved to Lana's son, Trey, who held a guitar in his lap. He'd grown so much in the last few years, soon he'd be taller than Lana. Her thoughts went to Jess, a teenager who'd stayed with them for a while before heading off to college. She wondered how he was doing, along with his father, Mike. While Mike had wanted his relationship with Christie to go beyond friendship, it had become evident to them both that they weren't meant for each other. Last she'd heard, he'd met a woman in Midland, and they'd gotten engaged. Christie was happy for Mike.

Trey strummed the guitar, working on a song of his own. With his talent and work ethic, she could easily see him making a name for himself in the music industry. He had a great voice and often did solos at weddings and for other events.

Christie headed inside to where she heard Lana humming a hymn. Curtis was also there.

"Howdy, Chrissy. Good to see ya." He nodded before saying goodbye to Lana.

"Is he not staying for lunch?" Christie sat down her bag.

"He'll be back." Lana pulled a crispy chicken leg from the frying pan and set it on a plate covered in paper towels. "If you can set the table, that would be helpful."

Christie went to the table, which was covered with the kid's papers, a bowl of fruit, and a bag that overflowed with paperbacks. Christie picked up one of the books that had fallen out of the bag. She held it up. *Her Second Chance*, and some others with the titles containing the word cowboy in them. Christie held up the books.

"Seriously?" She made a funny face.

"What? Everyone needs a little romance in their life." Lana replied.

"Okay, whatever." Christie rolled her eyes before shoving the books back into the bag.

Lana turned from the stove, tongs holding a crunchy chicken thigh. "Even you, Christie."

"No. Not me. I live in the real world."

"Romance *is* the real world." Lana set the thigh down next to the leg. She brushed off her hands on the apron she wore before stirring a pot boiling on the stove.

"Um, keep dreaming." Christie finished clearing off the table before wiping it down with a clean, wet washcloth. She pulled out the plates and set them in the places around the table.

Lana came over and added a stack of silverware to the table. "Have you ever been on a date in your life?"

"Don't be silly. Of course, I have. Plenty, actually." Christie set her hands on her hips. "What are you implying? That no one has ever asked me out on a date? Well, they have." She fumed.

"Well, I don't know what plenty is, but I know that since I've known you, you haven't gone on a single date." She moved back to the next batch of chicken frying in the pan. "I thought maybe you and Mike were going to go somewhere with your relationship, but that fizzled out."

"I could say the same for you."

"I can't help but hold up every guy to the man I married. It's hard for me to let go. I know it's not time for me yet as I must have some healing to do with his passing. I look at Trey and I wish his father were here to support him in his new pursuits. I wish he were here to share with Allie how a man should treat her." Tears sprung to

Lana's eyes.

"Oh no, now I've gone and done it. I'm sorry Lana. Sometimes I don't think, and I shouldn't have said anything."

"It's okay. It's just that you can't corral grief. It's like a wild horse that you think you've got under control until it bucks you off the saddle." Lana picked up a tissue from a nearby box and wiped her eyes with it, stuffing the wadded paper into her pocket. She took in a deep breath. "Let's not get all maudlin, okay?"

"Okay. It's not that I have any objection to dating." Christie set the silverware on napkins next to each plate. "I've just been busy. I was caring for Pop after his accident, then building my house, and now with Horse Haven, I don't have time for anything else."

"Oh, stop. That's just an excuse. You don't go anywhere where the men aren't Curtis' or Pop's age."

"Well, I'm trying to find me an old guy with his foot on a banana peel that leaves me billions of dollars." She winked.

Lana pointed the tongs at C.
couldn't care less about money. But y
get out and meet some guys your own a
old are you again, a hundred?"

"Ha. Ha. Hilarious. You should do stand-up comedy." Christie moved around the table, adding glasses to each place. "If I wanted to date, then I would. But I don't and you can't make me. So there." She stuck out her tongue at Lana.

"Hm. Well then, I'm just going to pray that God sends you the right guy."

"Oh stop. The only way would be if he walked in my front door. And you know that's not happening." She grinned wide. Other than showing Curtis, Lana, and the kids the house when it was finished, Pop was normally her only visitor. She liked how she felt set apart from the world, as if she were living in her own little eagle's nest, safe from the world. "Plus, I'm not changing my name either. Sorry, not sorry." She shrugged. "So, there you go."

"Okay, then. You asked for it." Lana turned back to the stove, humming again.

Christie shook her head at the young woman. However, she was glad that Lana had admitted how careful she was being about not bringing in anyone that wouldn't be great with her kids too. Christie admired Lana for her perspective and her life and work ethic. She was also glad that they had grown close over the years, like a younger sister that Christie had always desired.

The door opened and everyone piled into the kitchen, where talk centered on the rapid community's out-pouring of support for Maria and the kids. They also talked a bit about the nonprofit, and the upcoming gala. After they'd shooed everyone out of the kitchen and they'd finished washing up, Christie hugged Lana before heading home. Pop and Curtis were already stretched out in the front of the television, a football game on while they both snored in their chairs. Lana grinned and rolled her eyes at the pair, but Christie knew she loved the family as much as she did. Lana walked Christie out to her truck.

"You know what my favorite month is?" Lana

quipped.

"No idea. Which one?"

"March. As that means no more football games!" She chuckled.

"I hear ya on that one. I have to say that's one of the best things about being in my own place—not having to listen to the football games on the weekends. I don't mind them, but not all the time."

Lana hugged her. "See you tomorrow. I'll be late as the kids have a book fair at school and I volunteered to help out."

"Seems kind of close to the holidays for the fair, isn't it?"

"We actually planned it that way. Sent home information to the parents about giving the kids money for books as part of their presents. We'll see if it works out for us."

"Good idea. I like the idea for the auction items for the gala too."

"Don't forget. You have to donate one of your pies as one of the items. What are you planning on making?"

"Not sure yet. Trying to think what would work for it."

"Well, it is close to Valentine's, so maybe that will help with what you choose."

"Good point. It gives me an idea. I'll work on it sometime this week." Christie slid behind the wheel of the driver's seat, and Lana shut the door before waving goodbye.

Christie drove home, thinking about the type of pie that would work for the gala. She was lost in thought as she parked and then made her way up the wooden stairs to the house. She opened the door and was instantly enveloped in the quiet. She stood there, her hand on the doorknob.

Quiet was good, right?

But after all the chatter with Lana and the kids, the quiet felt stronger. Being alone didn't mean you were lonely. In fact, it was in crowds or with a bunch of people that any loneliness tended to rear its head where she was concerned. She moved over to the computer and fired up her music playlist, allowing the melody to cleanse any feelings. She sang along to the tune as she hung up her coat, before unzipping and sliding her feet out of the heeled boots she'd worn. She set them down next to the bootjack remover. It would be nice to have someone help take off her boots sometimes, she chuckled to herself.

Lana had provided a plate of leftovers for later, and the bag she'd set down had fallen over on the table next to the door. Picking up the bag, she walked over and set it down on the kitchen island. She pulled the plate from inside and stuck it in the fridge before going back to gather the other items from inside its depths.

A chuckle escaped her lips. Lana had snuck *Second Chance* into the bag when she wasn't looking. She threw the book onto the table next to her chair and finished putting the rest of the items back into her bag. After stealing a bite from the covered plate, she re-arranged items in her fridge for the leftovers.

Christie changed out of her other clothes, donning an old sweatshirt and a pair of baggy, flannel pants. Starting up the woodstove, she was thankful she'd taken the time to create a shelter for wood up on the deck area. It was a good thing that she didn't have to worry about wood as it was plentiful on the property, though hauling it upstairs wasn't as fun. The crackling of the fire felt like a warm embrace as she enjoyed the flames taking hold of the kindling. Warmth radiated out from the stove and Christie filled a kettle, placing it on top of the stove to boil water for a cup of herbal tea.

She hunkered down in her chair, picking up the nonprofit best practices book and a notepad. She clicked on her pen, ready to take notes, but found herself gazing into the fire, watching as the flames licked at the wood. The fire crackled in the hearth, mesmerizing her with its dance of flame. Her eyelids lowered, and she pressed her head against the chair-back, allowing herself to do something she rarely did, simply rest. Doing nothing was an area that she struggled with much of her life, never sitting still, always feeling the need to be doing something. But for now, the flames lulled her. She sighed.

Okay, that was enough relaxing for the

month. She knew she'd grow anxious if she didn't do something.

She padded over to the kitchen to work on meal prep for the following week. She put beans into the instapot and set to work chopping ingredients for salads and stir-fry. After putting them into mason jars, the beans were done, and she transferred them to another dish before restarting the pot with rice. She also cooked up hamburger she'd use to create a shepherd's pie and for tacos.

Once everything finished, she cleaned the kitchen, wiping down the counters and the stovetop. As she swept the floor, she gazed outside to where night encroached on the land, and darkness crept onto the deck. That's the one thing she hated about going into winter. She hated the dark coming so early. Flipping through various channels on the television, she groaned her way through terrible show after show, not finding anything appealing or worth watching. Giving up on watching anything, she switched the television off and as she set down the remote, her eyes fell on the fiction paperback Lana had snuck into her bag.

Well, it couldn't hurt to at least take a look. She made herself a cup of tea and opened the book.

CHAPTER FIVE

Monday morning arrived, and she, along with Lana, had a talk with all the volunteers and staff about safety. A note on her desk let her know that the electrical contractor would be sending someone else over to finish the lighting for the gala. A number was also left for her to use if she had any concerns or questions. She set it aside to call later and find out about Gabe's funeral, as well as any news on any of it.

Finally able to catch her breath, Christie looked up the number for the coroner's office. Just as she punched in the number, Alice opened the door, letting her know the caterer had arrived. She cancelled the call and followed Alice downstairs where a team of individuals were setting up tables. A woman in a chef's jacket, her midnight black hair cut short in a cute, modern pixie, made her way toward the table, holding a box.

"Can I do anything? Do you need help?" Christie asked.

The woman set the box down before replying. "Nope. We've got it." She held out her hand, "I'm not sure we've actually met. I'm Julie."

Christie took the offered hand. "Nice to meet you."

Julie removed a lid off of an insulated box and started placing containers onto the draped table. "I spoke with Lana, and she said a lot of the volunteers leave after one, so we wanted to get here early so everyone can have a chance to grab some lunch." She pointed to a man who was holding a pair of stacked boxes. "Those can go over there, where we'll set up the drinks station."

"This is genuinely nice, but you certainly didn't need to do this. Though it's much appreciated."

"I often do tastings before any event, and since Lana let me skip that during the holidays plus allow me my normal week off, I wanted to do something nice for you all. Especially after—" She hung her head, composing herself. "I was so sorry to hear about Gabe. It never should have happened to him."

"Yes, it was a tragic accident. He's got little kids at home, and it has to be devastating on them and Maria."

Julie took a deep breath. "Does this mean that you'll fire Bryson Electric and have another company come in and finish the work for the gala?" She pointed toward the ceiling.

Christie's brows knit together. "Why would I do that? It was an accident."

Julie shrugged. "Just a question. Safety is so important and someone else could have also been hurt. A member of staff, a volunteer, even an animal being boarded here."

"I guess, but we don't have animals in this barn. It's only used for office space and events like we'll be having in February."

"That's awful nice of you, as I'm sure this will affect your insurance."

Christie wasn't sure how to respond to this conversation, which had taken a strange turn. Julie yelled over at someone, "No, not there. Place those over here."

She turned back to Christie. "Sorry, I didn't mean to speak out of turn. As a business owner, I'm extremely vigilant on safety and so many other things as it can impact my business. Forget I ever said anything. I hate to be rude, but if you'll excuse me, I need to supervise this new crew."

"Not rude at all. Certainly, something to think about. I'll let you get back to your work. Just let us know when you're ready for everyone and we can announce it over the loudspeaker system."

Julie faced Christie. "You have a loudspeaker system?"

"Yes, we figured it would be easier than trying to hunt people down when they're needed." Christie pointed to the mechanical room when a thought came to her.

"Um, I heard you were here yesterday. Did you happen to see anything?"

Julie crossed her arms across her chest and shook her head. "See anything? Like what?"

"Just wondering if anyone may have any insight into what happened to Gabe. But you were here yesterday. Correct?"

Julie cleared her throat. "I came to see where to set up these tables. Why do you ask?"

"Again, just trying to figure out what happened yesterday. That's all." Christie swiveled as voices came to her ears. The board members had arrived for the lunch and to discuss the insurance issue after Don had sent out an email over the weekend after conferring with Lana.

"Hello everyone. Julie and her team are setting up, and she'll let us know when the food is ready."

Carol spoke to Julie. "Nothing with peanuts or peanut butter, is there? I'm allergic."

"Me too." A deep voice made Christie turn in its direction. A tall man with a mop of brown wavy hair and the shadow of a beard stood next to the doorway.

Christie heard a sharp inhale from one woman behind her. She swiveled to look, wondering what had caused the reaction but couldn't determine who had made the noise. She faced back to the man.

"I'm sorry. Can I help you?" She gazed up into warm brown eyes that met her own.

He pulled the hardhat from under his arm.

"Oh, you're with the electrical contractor? We need to speak with you. Could you join us upstairs?"

He nodded. "Sure thing. Hi Becky. Good to see you."

Was it her imagination or had a tension settled over the group? And if so, why? Julie was busy with her back to the group setting up the catering table while Carol had walked off and Bob and Amy had disappeared to one of the other horse barns.

Christie turned back to the contractor. "I'll call Lana over. Don, if you can join us in the meeting room, that would be great."

The man turned to the remaining group, "Ladies, gentlemen. Becky."

Christie turned to see Becky looking toward the ground. Did Becky know the man? He obviously knew her, as he'd called her out by name. She led them upstairs and offered them drinks before Lana joined them.

Up in the office, people grabbed coffee from a nearby kitchen before settling in behind the conference table.

"So, I'm sorry, I didn't catch your name."

The man raised his hat. "Bryson."

"Oh, okay. I apologize. I didn't know you were the owner. Now, Mr. Bryson—"

"Just call me Bryson."

"Fine." Why did she feel flustered by him? "Bryson, first, we're deeply sorry about Gabe. We want to help in any way that we can. We don't believe that we are at fault for any—"

"Whoa, there." He held his hands up. "Is this a meeting to go over the contractual deadlines or to stage an intervention?"

Christie huffed. "Well, I certainly didn't mean any offense. We simply need to know where we stand. That's all. As the nonprofit's executive director and as members of the board, we need to be cognizant of our fiduciary responsibility in case there is to be any litigation. Personally, I'd rather know if there is going to be anything from your company sooner rather than later."

He leant back in his chair, crossing his arms across his chest. "That's a lot of big words being tossed around. Now, until we hear from the medical examiner on cause of death, there's nothing to discuss. I will say—to ease your mind— that Bryson Electric has no current intention to pursue any form of litigation. Better?" He gave a lazy smile.

"Well, I—" Christie flushed.

Thankfully, Lana cut into the conversation. "I think we're all on edge due to what happened to Gabe. As you can imagine, anything that happens here can have a significant effect on us as we already exist on an extremely tight budget. If donors feel that their money isn't going to the horses and more toward claims or higher insurance rates, this could cause us to shut our doors."

"I like what you all are doing here. That's why I gave you such a cut rate for the lighting we're doing for the gala. Gabe's death was a terrible tragedy, but it doesn't look to be anything more than that. If you would like to do something for his family in his memory, I'd be happy to connect you with them."

"Thanks. Now, when do you think the lighting for the tables and stage area will be completed?" Lana interjected.

"If everything goes to plan, I think another week should do it. I'm here because I wonder if we might work in the afternoon or evening. That way, there aren't so many people around, and I think it will be better for the crew as well."

Christie thought about it. "I think we can manage that. It would certainly work better for us as well. When would you want to start that?"

"This evening? I'll come by and line out the new guys. Say six?"

"Okay. I can bring in some bar-be-que around five. That way, the guys don't have to worry about dinner."

"That's mighty nice of you. But certainly unnecessary." Bryson replied.

"I'll have to be here, anyway. Tom, our night security guard, is away until later and we have to have someone on staff on the premises. I can get some work done and I'll have to eat as well, so it's no trouble."

"Great. Anything else?" He stood.

Christie looked at Lana and then turned to Don, who'd remained silent during the discussion. "Don, anything to add or ask?"

He shook his head as a knock came on the door. It was Alice, followed by Julie, the caterer. "Lunch is ready if you'd like to come down now."

"Great. Bryson, please join us." Lana responded and motioned for him to follow her. They left the room and Christie turned to Don.

"What is it, Don? You're awfully quiet."

He shook his head. "I still think we need more insurance. It's all fine and good for him to say they won't pursue any litigation, but you never know, and we don't want to be caught on the back foot."

"I have to agree with you. While we certainly didn't do anything, it was on this property and that alone makes it where they could sue for damages for the family. Please check into more insurance, though I doubt that will help us now since the incident already occurred."

"True, but if something else were to happen-"

"Don't say that and jinx us, Don." She knocked on the wooden table.

He held up his hands. "My bad. Just saying. Better safe than sorry."

She sighed because she knew that his words were true. After all, that was the point of insurance. You got it, hoping you never had to use it, but were thankful you had it.

"I'm starved. Let's get down there and join the crew."

Downstairs, the board had arrived, and everyone was filling their plates or taking a seat on some hay bales that had been set up as seating. The table was laden with a salad, small strips of fried chicken, fajita meat, corn, and flour tortillas, as well as various salsas and dressings. At the end of the table, a display of petit-fours and chocolates were displayed in a heart-shaped Valentine's box.

"Looks delicious." Bryson spoke to the caterer before furrowing his brow. "Do I know you?"

Julie tucked a piece of black hair behind her

ear. "Well, um,—"

Carol interjected. "Do any of the cakes or anything else have peanuts in it? I'm allergic to them."

Julie shook her head. "Nothing. We are incredibly careful about that as so many people are allergic now to so many things. As you can imagine, it makes life interesting when you're a caterer nowadays." She smiled and busied herself tidying up the table.

Lana noted that Julie hadn't ever really responded to Bryson's question. How did Bryson know her? Probably another job where their paths had crossed. Christie waited until Carol and Lana had filled their plates before she turned back to the table. A commotion sounded behind her.

She swiveled to see Carol scratching at her throat. Hives had appeared and fear played on her face.

Bryson dropped his plate and rushed over to the panicking woman. "Where's your Epi-pen?"

Carol grabbed at her pocket and Bryson took it from her, stabbing the woman in the thigh with it. He yelled over his shoulder, "Call an ambulance!"

Christie pulled her phone before seeing Alice speaking into the phone with emergency services.

Bryson knelt down next to Carol, speaking calming words as he held her head. "It's all okay, now. You're going to be fine. Just calm your breathing. That's it. In. Out. Easy does it."

Christie went to Carol's plate. One of iced white cakes had a bite out of it. She went to the table and saw the cakes dusted with cocoa powder. "Julie, could the cocoa powder have gotten mixed up with something else?"

"Cocoa powder? What are you talking about? I didn't put—" She stopped when she saw the cakes. "What the?" Her voice trailed off as she wet her finger and touched the powder to her lips. "No, it can't be!"

Christie raked her finger over the light brown powder and touched it to her tongue. "Peanut butter."

Julie fought for composure. "There's no way that I, or any of my staff, sprinkled peanut butter powder onto those cakes. Someone here had to have done it." Her voice rose, frantic.

"Well, that was a close one." Bryson responded. "I'm allergic too."

"Everyone, please move away from the table." Christie raised her hands, and everyone stepped back behind the circle of hay bales, leaving only Bryson cradling Carol in his lap.

As she looked at the pair, a thought passed through Christie's mind. Who had been the intended victim—Carol or Bryson?

CHAPTER SIX

After the paramedics had taken Carol off to get checked out, Christie sat in her office, her head in her hands. While she didn't know of anyone that had rsvp'd for the dinner to have any specific allergies, she wouldn't want word to get out about this second incident.

She picked up the phone as it rang. It was Pop. "Hey, girlie. Sorry, I missed your call earlier. I was out playing dominos with Curtis and some other pals."

"Hi Pop."

"What's the matter?" Pop could always tell by Christie's voice if there was something wrong.

"We had another accident—well, I don't think this was an accident, so that makes me wonder if Gabe's death was an accident, but maybe they're not related, and—"

"Whoa. Slow down. Tell me what happened."

Christie related the events of the lunch to Pop,

who let out a slow whistle. "Scary. Good thing that Carol had that pen in her pocket. That could have turned out a lot worse."

"Yes, thankfully, she'll probably be okay." Christie sighed. "Pop, I don't know if I'm cut out for all this responsibility."

"Why would you say such a thing? Of course, you are. You're one of the smartest people I know besides myself, of course."

"Pop, you always make me laugh." She sat back in her chair, swiveling back and forth in it. "Listen, the electric company is going to work on the lighting for the gala in the evenings. That way, they don't have to work around others. I'm going to have to be here tonight to lock up, so I'm going to bring in some bar-be-que. You want to come over and keep me company while I work?"

"Sure. Can't say no to some good grub."

"Great. Well, got to catch up on some work, but I'll see you later." Christie ended the call, but the idea of getting into any online work wasn't appealing. She needed to work off some of this physical energy. She got up from her chair and grabbed her chambray and fleece jacket. After telling Alice she was going over to the other horse barns, she made her way to a stall. An older mare greeted her. "Hello, Sally. How's about a stroll in the yard?" Christie opened the stall door and fastened a simple harness over the horse's neck. "Ready?" Sally was known for her slow pace, but the crisp air invigorated Christie as they stepped out of the barn. She led Sally around the circular corral, letting the horse take the lead on the pacing. When they neared the entrance back to the barn, Sally pressed on, taking another lap around the dirt. "Feeling good today, huh, old girl?" Christie stroked the horse's muzzle. They finished a third lap before Sally stepped back into the barn's entrance. Back next to her stall, Christie brushed Sally down before leading her into the stall and rewarding the mare with an apple. Still filled with nervous energy, Christie wished she'd have brought extra clothes as she could expend some time mucking out stalls, but since she had to stay into the evening, she decided against it. She couldn't procrastinate her office work any longer, so she made her way back to the offices over in the adjacent barn.

Messages laid on her desk let her know that Carol was fine and had been sent home to rest. Another message was from the coroner's office. Finally, one was from Don saying he'd gotten a quote on an umbrella policy that he thought would work for them.

Christie hung up her jacket and then went to the bathroom to wash her hands. On the way, she passed the mechanical room. Instinctively, she reached for the handle, but the door swung open easily. She sighed. Hadn't she said to keep this room locked? She'd need to have another talk with Alice because of the recording equipment.

The recording. She needed to view today's video. Maybe someone could be seen tampering with the cakes. She took out her set of keys and locked the door, checking to see it was secured before heading to the bathroom. As she washed her hands, her mind played over the events of the last few days. Was someone trying to stop Bryson Electric from finishing the lighting? But why? Or was someone trying to cause problems for the nonprofit? The worst scenario is that someone was trying to kill Bryson. None of these were good. Once Tom returned, they needed to see about how they could up the security.

But first she needed to place the order for the bar-be-que at Fritze's. Then she could pick it up on her way to drop off the day's bank deposit. After placing her order for the large family meal of chopped beef, pulled pork and jalapeno sausage, she started answering emails when she remembered the coroner's call. She picked up her phone and called him.

After being put on hold, Christie held the headset between her head and shoulder as she typed on the computer. Finally, the coroner came on the line.

"Hi Christie. I wanted to let you know what happened to Gabe." His voice was low and somber.

She stopped typing mid-sentence and adjusted the phone to where she was holding it with her right hand. "Yes?"

"He died of trauma from the fall, but it was most likely that electrocution caused him to fall."

"What?"

"From what we can determine thus far, he was working with some live wires and either he stumbled, or he touched some metal and it knocked him off the ladder."

"I'm not sure, but wouldn't he have turned off the power for that?"

"I'm not an electrician, but yes, in most cases, they're not working with live wires. Someone must have turned the power back on to the circuits he was working on, and he didn't know it."

"But why would someone do that?"

"I can't answer that for you."

"Have you spoken with Bryson about this?" Christie cradled her hand in her chin.

"Yes, he told me to let you know too as he knew you were concerned of its effect on the nonprofit."

"So, can we rule out murder?"

"Not necessarily. Someone could have known that the power was off and turned it back on intentionally. Or they could have done so, not realizing that someone was working with the power. Conversely, Gabe could have forgotten to turn off the power or decided he could do the work he needed with the hot wires. If someone messed with the ladder he was on—regardless of whether on purpose or not, he could have grabbed for stability and that's what caused him to fall."

Christie rubbed her forehead as the beginning of a headache made itself known. "What are you labeling the death? An accident?"

"At this stage, it's being noted as undetermined. While it's a tragic accident, we can't rule out foul play."

Christie moaned. "Well, thank you for calling and letting me know."

"Before I let you go, I think I heard that you used to be a hospice nurse, is that correct?"

Her brow furrowed. "Um, yes."

"You've also helped bring a killer to justice. Actually, more than one."

"I'm not sure what this has to do with Gabe."

"I'm not going to beat around the bush. I have

a staffer who will be retiring soon, and I'll like you to consider filling the position."

"What?"

"Why not? You're more qualified than many of the others who would apply. You don't have to have any medical background for the position, but with your medical knowledge around death and your keen insights, I think you would be the best person to fill this opening. I know you. I know your work ethic. I think you'd be a great addition."

"I can't—"

"Don't say anything now. Just think about it. I'll be happy to chat with you more about it when you're ready. Ciao."

Christie stared at the phone. What in the world had just happened? She'd learned that Gabe's death was suspicious enough that the coroner wouldn't rule it as an accident. That he wanted her as part of his staff was out of left field. Work with the coroner? And weirdest of all, he ended his conversation with Ciao.

She bent over, tapping her head against the desk when Alice walked in. "Bad day?"

"You could say that. How do you remain so calm through everything, Alice?"

Alice shrugged. "I don't like conflict or confrontation. If I can minimize it, I do. That's why I make a good administrative assistant."

"You're right there. You're the calm in the constant storm that surrounds this place."

"Anything I can do for you before I leave for the day?"

"I noticed that the door to the mechanical room was open. Did you lock it?"

Alice paled. "Yes. Though...Um." She hemmed and hawed while Christie waited for her to continue. "I left my keys on my desk. I wasn't even thinking about anyone going in there. I'm sorry."

"It's fine. But in the future, make sure you keep your keys either on you or somewhere that no one could take them. Okay?"

"Okay." Alice gave a wan smile. "I'm sorry. I won't let it happen again."

"It's fine. I think I'm just wound up with Gabe's death and now Carol's issue. I wonder if we should hire another caterer just to be safe?"

"No!" Alice yelped before collecting herself. "Sorry. I just don't think that's fair to Julie. I know Julie didn't do it. Either by accident or on purpose."

"How do you know that?"

"I just know. Please don't fire Julie."

"Okay, but we need to be prepared for pretty much anything going forward."

Alice let out a low sigh. "I'm going to see Carol. Anything I need to let her know?"

"Let her know that she's in our thoughts and prayers. We'll figure out what happened."

"Okay, I will." Alice made to close the door.

Christie smiled at her. "You're a good friend to Carol. How long have you known each other?"

"Since high school. We became pals then."

"Well, she's got a good friend in you. Plus, I appreciate your recommending her to us for the board. She really gives good insights into the equine therapy program, and it's taken off in the last few months."

"She loves being here. It gets her out of the

house and away from the kids for a while." Alice placed a hand over her mouth. "Oh, I shouldn't have said that."

"Why not? I can't imagine having five kids, homeschooling, plus one with special needs. She deserves some time away for herself. While it may not be very relaxing here, as least she have some conversation with other adults."

Alice nodded, "Yes, you're right. I'll remind her of that when I talk to her. Well, see you tomorrow."

"I'll walk out with you. I need to go pick up bar-be-que for tonight." Christie gathered up her jacket. "Oh wait, I forgot something. Go on ahead and I'll see you tomorrow." She waved as Alice walked down the exterior hallway toward the steps down into the barn. Christie remembered that she hadn't looked at the video recording from today and she didn't want to wait any longer. She tossed her jacket down on the chair in her office and pulled her keys from a carabiner she wore on her jean's belt loop.

Unlocking the door to the maintenance room,

she made her way into the warm room. A monitor sat on the desk, and she opened up the program to look at the tape from the morning. This time, there was no denying the tape had been tampered with, as most of it was erased. Someone had once again ensured that the video footage wasn't available for viewing.

Christie folded her arms over her chest. She had to figure out who was able to get into the room and what had been on those tapes that they didn't want anyone to see. She shut down the monitor and rose from the chair. Her eyes went to the electrical panel on the wall. She opened it up and looked inside. Each area was numbered and lettered, so it was obvious if any areas were shut down. Had someone come up here, seen the breaker shut off and flipped it back on? That made no sense, as you had to open the door to even see the panel. Unless the panel had been left open. But that meant that person was also in the room. Was the person who'd flipped the breaker the same person who had erased the tape? Christie left the room and locked the door. Striding to her office, she placed a call to a locksmith.

She wanted that door re-keyed as soon as possible. If not today, then tomorrow.

CHAPTER SEVEN

The rest of the day passed quickly and soon Christie was saying goodbye to the nonprofit's volunteers. Lana had stopped by to chat with Christie when Bryson and three other men showed up. As Christie pointed toward the office upstairs where she'd laid out the food in the conference room, Lana twitched her eyebrows.

Christie made a face before asking, "What?" She pulled a pair of gloves from a back pocket and put them on, wiggling her fingers inside the stiff leather.

"He's really good-looking, isn't he?"

"Who?"

Lana shook her finger at Christie. "You don't fool me. You know who. He's a hunk."

"Oh, brother. Then have at him. Be my guest."

"Christie Taylor. You are the most oblivious person I know."

Christie set down a hay bale back on another

one. "What are you talking about?"

"He likes you."

Christie wiped her arm against her forehead to move her hair off her face. "Why do you say that?"

"Because I can tell when someone likes someone else. Like how Amy looks at Bob."

Christie grabbed another haybale and Lana grabbed the other side, setting it next to the others. "Bob and Amy...what are you talking about? Bob's married."

Lana shook her head. "Oh, ye of naivety. That doesn't mean anything to a cat on the prowl. Amy has her sights on him, or I'll eat my hat, and he doesn't seem to be pushing back awfully hard if he knows she's after him."

"Are you sure?"

Lana cocked her head, before retorting, "As sure as the moon's gonna come up."

"Wow. That's horrible." Christie shook her head. "What should we do?"

"Not much we can do. They're both adults. I just wished that Alice hadn't recommended her for the board."

"I didn't know that. So, Alice recommended Amy and Carol both?"

"Yep. It's before you agreed to come on as director."

The coroner's words sprang to Christie's mind. The last thing she needed to do was to add more on Lana's shoulders and burden her with Christie's leaving. It was true she'd wanted to back out of the position, but she hadn't planned to look until after the gala was done and dusted. She'd never even thought of that type of job and certainly never even imagined holding such a position. But being able to bring closure to families or even help bring their killer to justice made her consider it. She really needed to think it over. As she pushed her hair back off her face, Pop stepped inside.

"Well, howdy, Lana. Good to see you." He gathered her up in a bearhug.

"Pop, you always act like you haven't seen me in forever when you were just over on Sunday for lunch."

"That's practically forever. Plus, at my age, you get in all the hugs you can while you can."

Christie's heart clenched at Pop's words. She was certainly familiar with aging and death, but she didn't want to think about anything happening to Pop. If she had her way, he'd live until he was at least in his nineties. "Pop, I have the food up in the conference room. If you go on up, I'll join you in a minute."

"Sounds mighty good." He made his way up the steps, his stooped shoulders and gnarled hands revealing a life of demanding work.

Christie waved Lana off before stepping over to move the last haybale. Something caught her eye. It was a plastic baggie. Inside, it looked like light dirt or sand. She reached down to pick it up. Staring at it, realization dawned on her. She opened the bag. Sure enough, the smell of peanut butter rose to her nose. A knot formed in Christie's chest. This was proof that whoever had added the powder to the cakes had done so deliberately. She needed to chat with Bryson alone because it sure looked like someone was trying to harm him as she couldn't think of anyone that would want to harm Carol. Though she had to keep an open mind on who was the intended target. Conversely, someone have done it simply to cause problems for Julie. Or to cause worry over the gala's dinner. If that was the person's goal, they'd succeeded as this made Christie even more concerned about the food being served.

She carried the bag up to her office, dropping it into a bottom drawer. Should she call the coroner? Technically, the two incidents weren't related, or were they?

A text pinged on her phone. It was Orchid. Christie smiled as she thought of her artistic friend. Orchid wanted to let Christie know that she was done with the weaving for the gala's auction. Christie texted her back that she'd stop by tomorrow. After she locked her office, she went to the conference room, where the sounds of men's voices and laughter came through the closed door.

"Hello. Okay, for me to join in?" She smiled at

the men, whose plates held varying degrees of food.

Bryson rose, and as he did, all the other men stood. "Here, take my place. I'll move over here." He pulled his plate and large sweet, iced tea to another spot. Pop, who'd been making his plate, passed it over to her. "Here, take mine and I'll fix another one."

"Ya'll know how to make a girl feel special."

"Well, you'll always be special to me." Pop winked at Christie, who sat in the seat relinquished by Bryson. Pop added a heaping pile of potato salad before sitting down in another vacant seat. "Oh, I've been talking to Bryson about putting in some lights on your stairs."

"What?"

"You said something about it, so since he's here, I figured he might give us a quote."

"Pop, it's my house. I can get my own quote."

"Yep, but I'm the one that you don't want to fall down the stairs, so I should help pay for it."

Christie sighed. She knew there wouldn't be any point to stopping Pop once he set his mind to something.

Bryson wiped his mouth before speaking. "I told your father that we could easily add lighting on the stairs and some programming so it would come on automatically when the sun goes down and for it to go off after sunrise."

"Oh, I like that idea. Let me think about it. Now, is there anything I need to know to do or not do while you all are working here this evening?"

"Not that I can think of. This evening, the guys will finish what Gabe was working on, and then we'll move everything closer to the stage set-up. That's where we'll spend most of our time here. Don't worry. It will be ready for the gala."

The men rose and, after thanking Christie for the meal, left the room, leaving her with Bryson and Pop. She drug her fork through her food before committing to being straightforward in her approach. "Listen, I found a bag with peanut butter powder downstairs. That means someone brought it here on purpose." She swallowed and took a deep breath before continuing. "I think someone is out to ... harm you." Had that sounded better than kill or murder? She wasn't sure as she waited for his response.

He frowned. "What makes you say that?"

"Well, Gabe was driving a Bryson truck. He was up where his face would have been partially hidden. Then there's the peanut butter which you admitted today is an allergy. That's pretty coincidental, don't you think?"

He rubbed his hands on a crumbled napkin. "I can't say I'd considered that, but I don't know of anyone who would want to ...as you put it, harm me."

"What about Julie? You thought you'd met her before, and I found out that she was here when Gabe died."

"I don't know. I just felt we'd met. But that doesn't mean anything." He threw his napkin onto his empty plate, and Christie couldn't help but notice he wasn't wearing a ring.

"Do you know anyone here? I mean, on a more personal level?"

He grinned. "Why do you ask?"

Christie felt her face grow red with

embarrassment. "I only meant if there was someone who works here that could want you out of the way."

"I know quite a few here. Don is the one that contacted me when you first did the three quotes. I've bought most of my trucks through Bob, and I dated Becky years ago."

That was news. "Are you and Becky still dating?"

"Nah. We were just kids. I knew that I wasn't ready for the marriage, kids, and all that."

"Then you broke it off?"

He answered, "More like it was mutual. She got married to her husband, Phil. I was saddened to hear about his being killed by a drunk driver some years back."

"And you've stayed a bachelor?" Christie couldn't believe she'd just asked that aloud. She turned to see Pop staring at her with a smile on his face. She gathered herself. "Just thinking of anyone who might have it in for you or wants revenge for something."

"Well, there is one I can think of, but, naw."

He shook his head.

"Who? This could be the break we're needing."

"It's my dog, Hero. I did have him neutered."

Pop spat out his tea, as a loud guffaw escaped. He clapped his hand down on Bryson's shoulder. "You're funny, son. That was a good one."

"Funny, ha ha. I'm being serious here. Someone could be trying to kill you and you want to make jokes."

"Look, sorry. I didn't mean to make you angry. I don't believe that anyone is trying to do anything to me. Gabe's accident is tragic, but I believe it was just that, an accident. As for the peanut butter, that is weird, but I didn't tell anyone until after Carol had noted that she had an allergy."

Now that he'd said that Christie remembered that was true. She sighed. Nothing made sense. She wiped her mouth before picking up her plate and tossing it into the trash with the other plates. "I'm going to put the leftovers in the fridge. Pop, you staying?"

"I'm going to go down on the main floor and chat with Bryson for a bit. Then I think I'll head on home if that's okay with you, darlin'."

"Sure." She kissed him on the cheek. "Night Pop."

The pair walked out of the room, and Christie set to putting the leftovers away. There was enough that the staff could have some sandwiches tomorrow. She wiped down the table, all the while thinking about her conversation with Bryson. He didn't seem to think that anyone was after him. Maybe she was trying to fit pieces together that didn't belong in the box she'd created in her mind. She stepped out into the hallway and made her way to the landing. Bryson was laughing at something Pop had said. Most likely sharing one of his silly stories. He clapped Pop on the back, and the pair made their way outside.

Back in her office, Christie looked through the window to see Pop next to his truck, the pair in animated conversation. Finally, Bryson and Pop shook hands before Pop climbed up into the truck cab. She didn't know if Pop would see her in the window, but she waved as the truck's taillights lit up the dark. Turning back to her desk, she went to work on reviewing the month's donor newsletter. She was deep in concentration when a knock sounded on her door, causing her to jump.

"Come in."

Bryson entered. "Okay, all looks good. The guys have about an hour left, so I'm heading off. Thanks again for the dinner." He put the cowboy hat he held in his hand on his head. "See you later."

"Good night."

He closed the door behind him before a soft knock came on the door. She answered, "Yes?"

"Just so you know, I never married because I was waiting for the right woman."

Their eyes met for a brief moment before Christie glanced at her computer screen, trying to think of a response. Thankfully, she was saved from any reply, because Bryson tipped his hat and said, "Good night." The door shut, leaving Christie with a jumble of emotion.

Finally, she said aloud to herself, "Why do I

care why he's not married? It doesn't matter to me. I don't even know why he said that."

She put her focus back on the newsletter, adding in some pictures of the horses, volunteers and one of Carol's daughter during her equine therapy. Christie craned her neck and squinted. In the photo, Carol was chewing on her cuticles that were always ragged and red, her nails often bitten down to the quick. Her hair looked like it hadn't seen a brush in days. Christie lifted a quick prayer for Carol. She hoped this latest incident wouldn't be the last straw for the woman.

CHAPTER EIGHT

The next morning Christie texted Orchid that she would be stopping by, and she'd love to treat her to lunch at the Dodging Duck. Orchid responded with her normal burst of happy emojis. Jumping in the shower, Christie let the warm cascade of water envelop her. Her mind, as she'd tried to sleep, had been like a gerbil running on a never-ending wheel. Between the incidents, all the information concerning the upcoming gala that had to be checked and rechecked, and her confusion about going forward with the caterer, she'd tossed and turned until she'd finally fallen asleep. Then, for some unknown reason, Bryson's face kept popping into her mind. It must be due to her thinking that the incidents signaled someone with a grudge against him who might be seeking revenge. Yes, that had to be it.

After reluctantly turning off the water, Christie stepped from the shower and, after toweling off, wrapped up in her terrycloth robe. Then she got to work on her unruly curls. Using her fingers, she gathered up her auburn locks, scrunching them between her fingers. When she'd finished her work, she grabbed the towel Lana's kids had given her for Christmas. It was pink with the words about a little pony displayed on it. It still made her chuckle and smile when she used it, so she saved it for her hair since it would be no match against her tall, voluptuous figure. She pulled on fluffy slippers and made her way to the closet, where she pulled out a long-sleeved shift dress and a belt that clasped in the front.

She'd just sat down on a chair to pull on her boots when a knock sounded on her front door.

"Come in!" Christie rarely locked her door. Living out on Pop's property gave her a sense of security, along with the Sig in her drawer next to the bed. After a scary encounter not long after she'd moved back to Comfort, she'd grown more determined to learn all she could about gun protection and safety. Even going as far as to join the local A Girl with A Gun group. She'd also begun self-defense classes, so she could definitely protect herself if needed.

She heard the door open as she stood and went to the kitchen, pouring out a steaming cup of black coffee. "Morning! I've got you a cup here. I'm going to meet Orchid and we're stopping for lunch at the Duck if you want to join us."

Christie turned as Bryson stepped into view. "Oh! How did you get in here?"

He cocked his head as a lock of hair fell forward. "Um, the door. You said come in."

She sat the cup down on the counter. "Well, I thought you were Pop."

"Pop?"

"My father."

"Oh, yeah. Great guy."

Christie stared at Bryson until he held his hands up. "Um, do you want me to go outside, knock again, and you can ask who it is?"

"Don't be silly. You're already in here."

He glanced at the pink pony towel wrapped on her head before pinching his lips together to hide his chuckle.

Oh, no. She'd forgotten about the towel. Well, who cares? It didn't matter what he thought.

He pointed to the cup. "Coffee sounds good and since you already have it poured—"

She handed the cup to him, offering no cream or sugar. Moving past him, she went back into the living area. "What are you doing here so early?"

"I thought I'd get started on the lighting."

"What? I haven't even reviewed the quote." Christie replied.

"Oh sorry. He—your dad—told me he'd take care of the bill."

Christie fumed. She needed to let Pop know in no uncertain terms that she would take care of the bill.

"Well, that's not the case. So why are you here now?"

Bryson swallowed some coffee before answering. "His friend, Curtis, I think that's his name. Anyway, he's coming over and he invited me to join them. He said to swing by your place and look at the stairs for the lighting while I was at it."

Christie stifled the anger mounting in her chest. If Pop was trying to meddle in her life—

Her thoughts were interrupted by Bryson, who finished the coffee in one long gulp before washing out the cup and setting it in the sink. "Let's take a look at your ideas."

"Okay, fine. But I have to finish getting ready first. I'll meet you outside in a few minutes."

"Sounds good." He shut the front door that led out to the deck and stairs.

Christie walked into her bedroom, coming face to face with her reflection in the mirror next to the door. Oh no! She gasped at what she saw reflecting back at her. She'd totally forgotten that she'd put a face mask on while in the shower. Now the mask was cracked and green. Wetting a washcloth, she slouched off the mask, brushed her teeth, and released her hair from the towel. A tangle of riotous curls fell around her shoulders. She applied a moisturizer with sunscreen before adding tint to her lips, cheeks, and eyes with a color stick. Feeling better about the situation, she made her way out to the deck.

Outside, Bryson had pulled a tape measure from a pocket and was looking at the banister around the deck. "I like this house. Who designed it?"

"I did."

"It's really nice. I've always wanted a cob house. The idea about raising it up and leaving an area underneath for outdoor entertaining was smart."

Christie smiled at his sincere appreciation. "Thanks. Though I wasn't really thinking it through with Pop having to climb the stairs or for me later as I get older."

He glanced at her before responding. "I can tell you keep yourself fit and strong so I would think it would be quite a while before you'd need to worry about anything like that."

His compliments were getting to her, and she could feel a flush rising on her cheeks. She spun away and walked over to the stairs. "This is what I'm most worried about. Not just with Pop, but for anyone here at night, lighting would make it much safer."

"Do you have a lot of company at night?"

She turned to find that he'd moved closer to her. While still with plenty of space between them, Christie's mind went blank. "Um, well, no. I mean."

He turned away, and she felt relieved she didn't have to answer any more questions. She watched as he went over to the banister and noted that he could put lighting underneath as well as on each step. "I think it would enhance the safety because you'd not only see the steps, but the handrail would be illuminated as well."

"That's a clever idea." She nodded, liking his suggestion.

"Also, should you ever feel the need, it wouldn't be that hard to add an elevator from the inside of the patio area below to the upper floor. It'd cost ya an arm and a leg, but it could be done."

"Well, that's good to know. Though most of the time I usually go over to Pop's versus him coming here."

"Oh boy, I need to get going or I'll be in trouble." He moved to the side, and Christie moved to the same side. They repeated it on the other side. They laughed, and he surprised her by gathering her into his arms and dancing them around until she was on the other side of him. "If we're going to dance, might as well do it properly." He grinned, revealing a bit of a gap between his teeth, and Christie smiled back into his handsome, weathered face.

"Will I see you later at the rescue?"

He shook his head. "Not today. I've got plans for this evening. Maybe tomorrow." He jogged down the stairs and jumped up into the dually cab before heading off to Pop's house.

Plans. Of course, he had plans. Why wouldn't he? Just because he wasn't married didn't mean he wasn't dating. Christie stopped herself. No, it couldn't be. But she knew it was no use denying it. She was falling for Bryson.

~

Singing along to the radio, she arrived at Orchid's house in Boerne. The door was painted with a new moon with the new year in bold letters.

The background comprised many golden stars. As an artist, Orchid used her front door as a canvas, continually changing it to fit her mood or the season. People had begun driving by after the first of the month to catch a glimpse at her newest creation. Kids passed by loved to see the doors, and it was a natural occurrence to see kids and even teens taking selfies by it.

Christie had asked how Orchid could stand so many people coming around, but she often smiled and said, "The next best thing in the world is to make others happy. The first best is to make yourself happy. This makes me happy. It makes others happy. We can all use more happy."

Two people who couldn't have been more different, but their friendship had flourished. In some ways, Christie felt that Orchid took the place of her now gone mother. But it was deeper, and Orchid's insights always helped Christie to be less rigid in her thinking. Plus, with Lana so busy with the rescue, she needed a kindred spirit more than ever. While Christie and Lana enjoyed each other's company, Lana's life with kids differed greatly from Christie's kid-free lifestyle.

Christie got out of the truck and made her way to the unassuming rock house with the vibrant door. Orchid answered the door wearing large round glasses that eclipsed her face. Her hair was braided with gold ribbon and in the place of a beauty mark a gold star stood out against her skin.

"Wow. Orchid, you're stunning!"

"Come on in, honey. I'm almost ready." She held the door open for Christie, who couldn't wait to get in to see what Orchid had done to her front room, which was also changed whenever Orchid decided it was time. Today, the entire room was painted white, and even the floor was white. In the center of the room was a projector with the light on. Christie spied sheets of magenta, yellow, and green, but the ceiling was white.

"Why isn't the ceiling showing the colors?" Christie's brow furrowed.

"Oh, it is. White light is the inclusion of all the colors in the spectrum. It is clear and new. Just like the year we're beginning. I call this 'possibilities.' Now, follow me to the back." Orchid waved her hand, and they walked into the back room where a weaving was mounted on the wall. The colors and weave were tight and full at the top but as it moved down, it grew lighter and softer. Almost like a cloud. It was beautiful. "What do you think? Will this work?"

"Oh Orchid. It's gorgeous. Anyone would be privileged to have this piece of art."

"I'm glad you like it. It's not finished yet, though."

Christie drew closer. "It's not?"

"No. Something's missing. If you look, there are two strands of color at the top. I don't know if they should meet or go on straight. But it will come to me. Once that's done, it's yours."

"Wait, what?"

"It's for you. I've been meaning to give you something for your new home. I hope you like it."

"Are you kidding? I love it." She rushed over and gathered Orchid up in a hug. "I can't believe I'm going to have such a beautiful work of art in my home. I'll treasure it forever."

"There, see, you've given a gift to me in

return. Happy. Happy."

Christie grinned, "I love your optimism. I certainly could use some right now."

"Why, what's happened?"

Christie filled her in on Gabe's death and the incident with Carol. "I'm hoping that we don't have to go through the whole three things."

"The three things?" Orchid slipped into a woven jacquard jacket that was hung over a chair.

"You know. Like things come in threes."

"Ah, okay. Well, I'm ready. Let's get going. I missed breakfast, so looking forward to an early lunch."

"What about the weaving for the gala?"

"Not ready yet. No one gets to see it until the day of the event. Not even you." She winked, looking like an owl behind the thick glasses perched on her nose.

"All right. Let's get going." They drove over to the Duck, and because the weather was fairly nice, chose to sit outside. "Are you sure this isn't going to be too cold for you out here?"

Orchid responded, "No. Plus, it's good to get

some fresh air in the lungs. I'm perfectly fine in this jacket."

"It's so pretty. Where did you get it?"

"Oh, I made it." She ran her hand down one sleeve, a shimmering of color of various hues caught the light as she moved.

Christie thanked the waitress, who'd brought them hot tea. "I didn't realize you were a seamstress as well. That reminds me. I need to figure out something to wear to the gala next month. I may go into San Antonio and see what I can find. Any recommendations?"

"Yes." Orchid cupped her hand on the mug, the various rings she wore on her fingers glinting in the sunlight.

"Great. Where?"

"Not a where. A who. I want to make your outfit."

Christie struggled with her answer. She loved Orchid dearly, but she was much more subdued and couldn't imagine wearing anything remotely like the colorful outfits that Orchid sported. As she struggled with a polite way to respond in the negative, Orchid burst out with laughter.

"What?" Christie looked around to see what had captured Orchid's attention.

"Honey, you don't have to worry. I wouldn't make you an Orchid dress, I'd make you a Christie dress."

Christie blushed in embarrassment. "Orchid, I don't like the fact that you seem to read my mind."

"I can't read minds, but I know something else is on yours. What gives?"

The waitress came and set their plates in front of them, disappearing after asking if they required anything else. Christie dug into her meal.

Finally, she set down her fork. "I don't know. I feel, um, I don't know, not myself."

Orchid stared at Christie. "Oh, I see."

"What do you see?"

Orchid smiled a gentle smile and patted Christie's hand. "Now I understand the threads."

CHAPTER NINE

After she drove Orchid home, Orchid took Christie's measurements and sent her on her way. Christie then stopped home where she changed into jeans and t-shirt with a plaid shirt on top. She pulled on boots that would work for the barns.

She arrived at the rescue as Lana and some of the volunteers were helping with unloading horses that had been evacuated from a fire. She waved to Lana and let her know she'd come help after she dropped her things in the office.

Upstairs, Alice was engrossed in a spreadsheet. Christie waved and walked into her office where Bob was waiting. "Hey, Christie. I was hoping to connect with you before I had to leave. I just wanted to go over the sponsorship materials again. People can put up banners or signs outside of the barns the day of the gala, but sponsors of the evening will only be in the program and on the slideshow before the gala starts, correct?"

"Yes, we'll acknowledge the sponsors and

those who provide auction items, but it will only be in general. Can I help with anything, or do you have it handled?"

"All under control. We're even collecting at places around town for those who can't make it for the day's activities. It's a lot of work but I think it's going to pay off for us."

"That's great news. Now, if you'll excuse me, I have to check in with Alice on some other items."

He rose and shook Christie's hand. "You've done an excellent job. I don't know what we'd do without you." He picked up his coat and left the office leaving Christie alone with her thoughts. She did enjoy working with the rescue but is it where she was meant to be? Orchid's words came back to her. The first best person is to please yourself. Was she doing that by staying at the rescue or should she really consider the coroner position? Well, none of that mattered now. She walked back to where Alice was working. She looked up and smiled at Christie. "Hi ya. Just wanted to see if there were any updates on the Gala attendees. I think we're going to be at capacity. Pretty exciting for our first donor event."

"I agree. Bob says the sponsorships and general donations are good as well. Listen, I wanted to ask about Carol. Have you been in touch with her to see how she's doing? If we need to, she can certainly bow out of her committee assignment."

Alice shook her head. "Please don't do that. She needs that assignment. I think she's struggling a bit on being her own person besides being a mom. Her face lights up when she talks about her time here. What happened to Carol was foolish. It won't happen again."

"How can you say that? I found a bag with peanut butter powder in it. It could have been a lot more serious, even deadly."

Alice looked like a deer in the headlights. "I didn't mean—"

"I apologize. We have to take this seriously. Someone wanted to cause harm. Whether they meant it to be Carol or Bryson, or even someone else, remains to be seen."

"What about Julie?"

Christie pulled up a chair. "Julie? Does she have a peanut allergy too?"

"No. But it could be detrimental to her business. You even said that you were thinking of switching caterers."

"I'd never thought of that." Christie crossed her legs in the chair. "Certainly, something to think about."

"Or someone could be trying to shut down the rescue. We had that tragic accident with Gabe, then the one with Carol, we all know that dreadful things seem to come in threes."

"No, we're not going to have anything else happen. We don't even know if they were related."

Alice clicked on her keyboard to save her work. "True. I just think that it's important that we don't jump to any conclusions about anyone."

"I'm not jumping to conclusions. What makes you say that?"

"So you're not firing Julie?"

"No. You're right. It wasn't her fault that happened. She would be sabotaging herself if she added that to the cakes." Christie sat forward. "On another note, do you know how Bryson and Julie know each other?"

"No idea. I know he and Becky dated but it was years ago."

Christie wanted so badly to ask Alice if she knew if he was seeing someone now. Instead, she rose from her seat, saying, "Well, I'll let you get back to work. I've got a long to-do list waiting for me too."

"Are you staying here tonight again?"

"Yes, that's why I came in later. I thought I'd left a message about it."

Alice nodded, "You did, but I wasn't sure if that was the reason. I left some things in your in-box to look over. Don sent a quote for insurance, Julie called to confirm the menu still works, and that reporter called again. Her number's on your desk."

"Thanks Alice. I appreciate all your work."

"My pleasure." She turned back to her screen and began typing again.

After spending the next few hours on paperwork and catching up on calls, Christie decided a break was in order. She headed out to the adjacent barn where Lana waved her over.

"I thought you were going to come and help us out." Lana winked.

"Oh geez. Totally spaced that after I spoke with Bob and Alice. I'm sorry. Do you still need help?"

"Naw. Alice had called in a group of volunteers, so we had the help we needed." She set down a clipboard featuring the horse's vital data next to the stall. Rubbing the gelding's muzzle, she pulled a carrot from a bucket and gave it to the horse before strolling over to the next one on the list. "I spoke with Curtis earlier. He said that he and Pop had breakfast with Bryson this morning."

"Yes, I talked to him before he went over there to meet them."

"He called you?" Lana tilted her head, the ponytail bouncing behind her.

"No, he stopped by my house to give me a quote on lighting on the stairs."

"At your house?"

Christie moved a piece of tack to its hook.

"Yes, he came inside for some coffee. Why?"

Lana burst out laughing. "Wow, that was fast."

"What are you talking about? What's so funny?"

"Not funny." She snorted which only made her laugh more.

"Stop it! Now you're making me laugh and I don't even know why." Christie chuckled.

Lana doubled over, her contagious laughter causing Christie to join in with the woman who was wiping tears from her eyes. Lana would try to compose herself, point to Christie and go off into another laughing attack.

"Oh my gosh. My sides hurt now." Lana brushed her hands across her eyes again.

"You're such a goof. You had me laughing simply because you were laughing."

Lana grinned widely. "You still don't get it, do you?"

"Get what?"

"Answered prayers, Christie. Answered prayers."

~

That evening after everyone had left and the electrical crew were once again at work on the stage lighting, Christie had time to think about what Lana had said. It was simply coincidence. Lots of people had come through her door. Okay, well maybe not lots and no men other than Pop, Curtis, and Lana's son, Trey, since the house had been finished. Plus, she wasn't a spring chicken anymore. Men often fathered children long after women could bear children. And while Christie loved children, she hadn't ever felt that clock ticking. Now she was pretty sure that clock had stopped for her. Being an honorary aunt to Lana's kids was perfect.

Ugh. Why was she even going down this train of thought? She'd never felt the call to marriage, and she was content with her life. She flung on her coat and walked out into the night air.

The chill invigorated her. By the time she made it back into the primary office barn, the guys were packing up their gear for the night. She waved them off before locking up the doors.

The sound of metal falling came to her ears. She swiveled but behind her the space was empty. She went upstairs and phoned Tom. He was in the other barn in his apartment and Christie heard an action feature in the background. After telling him she was leaving for the night, she shut off her office lights. As she walked around her desk, she saw a figure dressed in black running from the barn. There was no way she could catch them. She called Tom back and he said he'd meet her out front.

Christie pulled her weapon from her holster and made her way down the stairs. While she didn't think anyone else was in there, she didn't want to be proved wrong. As she ensured that the bottom space was clear, she headed out into the night.

A figure rushed around the barn, and she took a stance with her gun, "Stop!"

"It's me, Tom."

She lowered the weapon and Tom pulled a large flashlight from his jacket pocket. They both scanned the arena, and around the barns but nothing looked amiss.

"What do you think, Tom?" She holstered her gun.

"Could it have been one of the guys coming back for some tools they'd forgotten?"

"I don't think so. Though if they'd put on a dark jacket, that could be possible. But why run away?"

"Maybe they didn't realize anyone would be here. Usually, this place is shut down tight for the night."

"That's true."

"I know we've talked about this before, but I think having a dog or two around at night would be a good thing. I have monitors where the horses are and some basic areas, but we don't have full control over security when I'm sleeping. A dog would alert me."

"I'm just worried about them around people and the animals."

"There are plenty that are trained and do fine around people and animals. We can keep them penned up much of the day, so they are more alert at night."

"I don't know. Pop's dogs, Mutt and Jeff may bark but they'll lick you to death if anything."

"Well, think about it. We've already had two terrible things happen in a brief amount of time. You know what that means."

"Not you too!"

"Just saying. I've seen it happen more than once."

"Well, we're not having it here. It's just a silly superstition. All is going to be okay and nothing else is going to happen."

"If you say so." His face showed his disagreement with her statement.

"I refuse to believe it. Bad things may come in threes. But maybe that was the third thing and now we can all get on with our business."

"Could be. Let me walk you to your truck. I don't think the person's still here but better to be safe."

Christie thanked Tom as he waited for her to get in the truck. He waved and turned back to the barn, most likely upset he'd missed a lot of the movie he was watching. But her mind was focused on what had happened.

Someone had come into the barn. While she didn't know what they were doing, it did make her wonder if the accidents were not against a particular person, but someone had it out for the rescue. If so, who was it and why?

CHAPTER TEN

Christie had felt relieved when Friday arrived and nothing else had occurred. They'd been able to break the curse of threes. She wanted to sleep in but found herself up at the crack of dawn as rain spat against her windows. So much for any ride with Champ. After morning chores, she came up to a nice warm house from the fire going in the wood stove.

She'd promised to make a pie for the gala's auction, and she wanted to test out an addition to the recipe. She pulled her recipe book out from the bookcase and sat down at the table. Before she started, she wanted to ensure she had all the ingredients. She would make two pies. One as the original recipe and one with the additional toppings. Then she'd get Pop, Curtis, Lana, and the kids to give her their input.

She washed down her counter again and laid down a heavy plastic for rolling out the pie dough.

After she'd made two shells, she set them aside and pulled out the rest of the ingredients. The rain was soft against the windows, enveloping her in a cozy cocoon.

The phone rang. It was Pop.

"Doing okay up there, girlie?" His gravelly voice came through the speaker.

"Yes, Pop. I'm high and dry up here."

"Just wanted to check on you and make sure you were okay."

Christie wiped her hands on a wet cloth. "Thanks for thinking of me. How are you doing?" She washed the plastic pie sheet and put it in on the sink drainer.

"If I were any better, I'd be two of me."

"Good. Still on for stew later?"

He replied, "Yep. You come on over whenever you want. I'll be here."

She pulled out her measuring cups and mixing bowls, setting them on her kitchen island. "Will do. See you later. Love ya Pop."

"Love you too."

The call ended. Christie smiled. Even though

she'd been on her own for over twenty years, her Pop always wanted to make sure she was okay. Having moved back to Comfort in order to be by him, it felt like he now had a new job to take care of her.

She turned on some of what she called her rainy day music and listened to the melody as she pulled out the items to make what she was going to call her Deathly Decadent Chocolate Pie.

~

Rich Chocolate Pie

Ingredients

3 large eggs

1 cup sugar (226.79 grams)*

3 cups milk (0.71 liter)

4 tablespoons flour (59.15 milliliters)

2 tablespoons cornstarch (29.57 milliliters)

2 ounces baking chocolate (get a good quality chocolate) (56.70 grams)

Prepared or purchased pie shell (makes one nine inch pie)

Tools Needed

    Mixing bowls

    Measuring cups

    Measuring spoons

    Double-boiler or pots that can be used as one

    Silicone Spatula or wooden spoons

    Mixer (If making meringue for topping)

Gather all your ingredients and read the entire recipe before beginning to cook your pie filling. Preheat your oven to 300 degrees or approximately 148.8 Celsius. Check your oven for conversion.

Step one: Melt the chocolate in a double-boiler on low heat. Keep an eye on it as you begin to make the custard portion of the pie. While it melts, move on to step two.

Step two: Separate the egg yolks from the whites. Save the egg whites if you are going to make a meringue topping for the pie.

Step three: Beat the egg yolks and add the one cup of sugar. Make a thin smooth paste by adding a little of the milk to the flour and cornstarch. Start with a small amount—a few tablespoons, adding a little more as needed to make the smooth paste, removing any lumps.

Step four: Scald the remaining milk in a pot. Don't burn. Use a wooden spoon to continue to move the milk so it doesn't burn on the bottom.

Step five: Stir a little of the scalded milk into the egg yolk mixture and the flour mixture. Stir until incorporated and then add each of these mixtures to the remaining scalded milk to create a custard. You add little amounts to each of the mixtures so that it doesn't clump which could happen if you add them directly to the primary mixture. Be patient and take your time on adding the mixtures together to ensure an integrated, smooth chocolate custard filling.

Step six: Cook over low to medium heat until

custard is thickened, stirring to ensure it doesn't burn on the bottom of the pot. You should be able to see and feel it start to thicken.

Step seven: Slowly stir the melted chocolate into the custard mixture until it is fully incorporated in the custard.

Step eight: Once thickened, add one teaspoon of vanilla. Stir until incorporated.

Step nine: Pour into prepared pie crust. Enjoy scraping the sides and eating that yummy chocolate goodness!

Optional: If desired, whip the egg whites into meringue and top the chocolate pie with meringue.

Bake the pie at 300 degrees (148.8 C)* for 15 to 20 minutes.

Use a toothpick in the center to check and ensure its firm. Cool.

Can be eaten warm (after baking) or cold.

Check to ensure these are the right conversions for you.

Meringue

Because this pie is sweet, you can simply use the whipped egg whites on top. However, if you prefer the traditional meringue, follow this recipe.

Ingredients

3 large egg whites

6 tbsp. sugar (88.72 milliliters)*

1/4 tsp. salt (1.23 milliliters)

1/2 tbsp. vanilla (2.46 milliliters)

Tools Needed

Mixing bowl

Measuring cups

Measuring spoons

Silicone Spatula

Electric Mixer

Step one: Put egg whites with salt into mixing bowl and beat until stiff.

Step two: Fold in the sugar gradually by using the spatula. Do not user the mixer once the whites are stiff.

Step three: Add in vanilla and using spatula, lightly fold again.

Step four: Using the spatula, top the chocolate pie with mounds of the meringue. Pull at the meringue to create peaks on the meringue.

Cook pie covered with meringue for 15 to 20 minutes. Check through the oven door to ensure that the meringue is lightly browned (only on the peaks) and does not burn.

Check to ensure these are the right conversions for you.

Christie's Deathly Decadent Chocolate Pie

Use the recipe for the Rich Chocolate Pie but do not use the egg whites to make the meringue topping. Let pie cool and put in refrigerator overnight. The next day, create the toppings for the chocolate pie.

Ingredients

3 3/4 cups confectioners' sugar, sifted

3 large egg whites

1 large can of cherry fruit filling for pies

Tools Needed

Measuring cups

Mixing bowl

Silicone Spatula

Mixer

Knife or metal spatula

Step one: Using an electric mixer, combine a small amount of confectioner's sugar with the egg white, whipping until mixed while continuing to add the confectioner's sugar. The mixture should be firm but spreadable. If it is too thick, you can add a bit of water or milk. If you don't want to use egg white, you use a flax egg or aquafaba.

Step two: Working with a warm metal spatula or knife, carefully spread the icing onto the cold chocolate pie. You may need to work in small groups while using a glass of warm water to dip the spatula in between each batch you're working on to help the icing spread easier onto the pie. Continue until the icing covers all the chocolate. Put back into the refrigerator until set. Because the pie is already cold, this shouldn't take long, but an hour or more will work best.

Step three: Before serving, open a can of cherry fruit filling and spread over the icing mixture. Return to the fridge to let set.

For serving, use a sharp knife to cut pieces of your pie. Once cut, you can let it sit at room temperature until you're ready to serve dessert. This will allow the icing layer to break down and liquify just a bit so that you have what is essentially a chocolate-covered cherry pie!

Cut into slivers or small wedges. If desired, can be accompanied by a small scoop of cherry gelato or vanilla ice cream.

As this pie is extraordinarily rich on the palette, recommend a strong coffee or black tea or milk to accompany it.

Enjoy!

~

Christie finished making the two pies. One would be plain chocolate with no topping and the other one would be full on sugar high. She washed up the dishes and was putting everything back in its place when she stopped in her tracks. She looked at the various ingredients still sitting on the island and wondered what had caused her to pause. Though she struggled with what her subconscious was trying to convey, it simply wouldn't come to the forefront of her mind.

Ingredients. What did it mean? Her mind refused to yield any other insights. She finished putting everything away before noting that the rain had stopped. It wouldn't be much longer, and she'd go over to Pop's for dinner, but for now, she curled up with her latest read. Soon her head was nodding, and she fell asleep on the sofa in front of the toasty fire.

When Christie woke, the fired had died down

with the remaining coals a mix of black and red. She rose from her chair and stretched before making her way into her bathroom where she washed her face. Outdoors she moved carefully down the steps, the dark boards now saturated from the rain. With the moisture still heavy in the air, she decided to take the truck instead of walking over to Pop's.

Wuss. She chided herself.

Warm yellow light blazed from Pop's windows and tear pricked at her eyes. A feeling of home and belonging enveloped her. She exited the truck, the frigid air full of humidity bringing a chill to her skin. She shivered as she rushed up the porch to hear the dogs, Mutt and Jeff, going crazy at the door. Christie barely got inside as they welcomed her with excitement, tails wagging.

"Ouch. Watch that tail, Mutt." She swiveled around, but the dogs continued their hearty welcome. "I'll pet you! Just let me get inside and close this door."

"Sit!" Pop's voice commanded.

The two happy dogs sat, their tails thumping

in unison on the wooden floor.

"You need to make them dogs behave. They'll run right over you if you let them."

Christie hung her jacket on the hook by the door. "Like you do? They've got you wrapped around their finger." She knelt and the two dogs happily accepted the pets and scratching of their heads and necks. "Ugh." She held up her hands, now covered with a layer of gold and brown fur. "I thought they were done with the shedding."

"Nope. They were done with the changing to winter coat shedding, now this is the getting ready for spring shedding."

Christie made her way into the kitchen, where she first wiped her hands on a paper towel, trying to dislodge most of the fur before washing her hands. Pop moved slowly to finish putting food in their bowls, along with a few pieces of the meat from the stew he'd made. The dogs gulped the food down greedily, like they were starving, as if they'd not eaten in months.

Christie finished setting the table as Pop scooped out ladles of stew with potatoes, carrots, and onions into heavy, ceramic bowls. He brought it to the table and set it down in front of Christie before bringing over the cornbread and setting the iron skillet down on a trivet. After a short prayer, Christie dug into the meal.

"Ooh, Pop. This is—" She took another bite. "Hm. I like it, but it tastes different. What did you do?"

"Added a bit of cinnamon. Saw it on one of them cooking shows so thought I'd try it. Like it?"

Christie responded, "Yes. It's good. Got any buttermilk?"

"Oh yeah. Forgot to put it out."

Christie grabbed the container from the fridge, pouring herself and Pop a glass before crumbling big chunks of cornbread into it. She scooped some out with a spoon. "This is heaven, Pop."

"Well, as your Mama used to say, 'You can't go wrong with simple food.' I have to agree with that." He speared a potato.

Christie saw the television on a stand in the corner. "Whatcha been watching, Pop?"

"It's about the Monarch butterflies. They travel down to this place in Mexico and winter there. It was showing it on a documentary I was watching. Pretty interesting. Ever heard of the butterfly effect?"

Christie knit her brows together. "I think so. Isn't that where things are supposed to change because of the butterflies' wings?"

He nodded. "It's often talked about with weather, but in the big picture it's how one thing changes another thing and so on."

Christie's phone beeped with a text. It was Don. Again.

"Need to answer that?"

Christie shook her head. "No. I'll respond later. Speaking of one thing changing another, Don wants us to get more insurance for the nonprofit. I've told him we can't discuss anything until after the gala is done and dusted, but he's adamant. To be honest, it's getting a bit annoying. I can give input, but it's really up to the board." She sighed. "I'm just not sure about this job. I did it to help Lana out, but the coroner is asking if I'll be part of his staff."

"Are you considering it?"

"Sure. I'll consider anything, but I'm not even going to think about it until after the gala. It's been so much work. If we had more help, it would be okay, but this has been a lot more work than I'd realized. Not just on me, but the staff and the volunteers. I'll be glad when it's over."

"Well, I'm mighty proud of all you're doing to help Lana, plus those horses. I know that when I'm let out to pasture, you'll take loving care of me when I'm no longer good for anything."

"Pop, don't say such things."

"Darlin, it's just the unpleasant facts. We live and we die. You don't need to worry about me kicking off anytime soon. God tends to take the good ones like your Ma first." His voice quivered for a second before he composed himself. "I'm so stubborn and ornery that He's probably waiting till the last possible minute."

"Pop, you are something. I'll give ya that. Now, let's get these dishes done and then how about a board game?"

"I thought you'd never ask."

CHAPTER ELEVEN

Christie arrived at the barn where she greeted the volunteers who were outside, unloading feed donated by Amy into wheelbarrows.

"Hey, Amy. How's it going?" She waved.

"Great. I was able to 'convince' my supplier to give me a good deal on feed if I bought extra and paid for the next order upfront." She made air quotes with her fingers.

"This is wonderful. I know it will help Lana's budget for sure."

Amy pulled off her leather work gloves. "Has Don been calling you? He wants to make sure I vote to approve that umbrella policy."

"Yes. I agree that we need to look into it, but it doesn't help with Gabe's accident. Plus, I can't think about anything else right now."

"Good to hear I'm not alone in wanting to wait until our board meeting in March."

A commotion sounded over at the barns. A

woman screamed. A dog barked.

A dog? What in the world?

Christie and Amy jogged over to where they could see a German Shepherd barking furiously, its hind legs poised to pounce. She felt a presence and turned to see Bryson.

"Oh, I'm so glad you're here. I don't know where that dog came from. I don't see any of our volunteers over there, but—"

"No, that's Hero." Bryson put his hands to his lips and whistled. The dog swiveled and ran back to Bryson's side but continued barking. "Hmm, something's not right. Ya'll stay back here just to be safe."

Bryson moved over to the bales, his shoulders tensed. The dog's barking grew louder. Reaching over behind a bale, Bryson pulled up a long snake, holding it behind the head with his gloved hand.

Amy cried out. "A rattlesnake!"

"Nope. Similar in looks, but it's just a bull snake." He looked at the snake. "How'd you get in here, fella?" He moved over to the exit door and strode outside. Hero sat at the door, waiting for

Bryson to return.

When Bryson came back inside, sweat dotted his forehead. "This weather. Cold one minute, hot and steamy the next." He pulled off his chambray jacket.

"Hot and steamy is right." Amy stage-whispered.

Christie's jaw dropped as she glanced over to where Amy was staring at Bryson. Did Amy carry a torch for Bryson? Or was she involved with Bob? Maybe there wasn't anything there between them and Lana had gotten it wrong. An emotion rose in her and it stunned Christie to realize she was jealous. When had she ever been jealous? Not anytime she could remember. She tamped down the rising emotion and crossed her arms, waiting for Bryson to join them. Hero tagged along, his eyes fixed on Bryson.

"You better come see this." He motioned to the pair to follow him back to where he'd found the snake. "The snake was put there on purpose. Look, you can see where there was a mouse, probably more. And the area's damp, so they were most likely frozen. That means they came from a pet shop."

Christie responded. "But why do something like that?"

"This." He motioned with his hand. "Let's say that you are over here working, and you see the snake which looks a lot like a rattler, what's the first thing you're going to do?"

Christie saw a shovel nearby, up against the wall. "I'd probably grab—"

"Wait." He snatched her hand. Christie felt a tingle go up her arm. Their eyes met briefly before he dropped it. "Look closer."

Christie and Amy moved closer to where Bryson stood.

Amy pointed. "Wait, what's that?"

"Either fishing string or floss. Look at this." He pointed out where the string went, which was to another stack of hay bales. "If you were to pull that shovel, it would start those bales falling. It's an accident waiting to happen."

"Oh, wow." Amy replied. "That would have been three accidents."

Christie shook her head, "No accident. Someone did this. The question is why they're after the rescue."

~

After saying goodbye to Amy, Christie turned to Bryson. "Thanks for helping out earlier. I'm glad we found the snake and the trap before someone got hurt."

"At your service."

She glanced down at Hero, the dog's tongue hanging out of his mouth. The chestnut brown eyes fixed on her. "Is he yours?"

"Yep. I had a buddy in the police department, and they were retiring Hero and Bitsy. Tom had cornered me the other day and was asking about getting some dogs for onsite here. I thought I'd bring Hero along so you all could see if this is what you wanted."

"I have to say, he looks pretty scary, and his bark is something else."

"You have nothing to worry about if you're one of the good guys. And I know you are." He smiled. "But he's not so nice to bad guys."

"Well, he saved our bacon today. We survive on the many volunteers we have. If someone were to get scared or hurt, no matter how little, it could stop others from volunteering."

"Well, glad I was here to save the day. Or at least Hero was."

"I'm glad you're here too." It was now or never. "I, well, I'd love for you to be my guest at the gala at our table. Of course, you can say no. There's no obligation to—"

"I'd love to. Dress code?"

"Basically, its Ballgowns and Boots is the theme."

"Gotcha. Fancy on the top, country on the bottom? Would a tux and jeans do?"

"Pretty much."

"What time should I pick you up?"

Christie blushed. "Oh, no. I'll be here early and will be staying late to clean things up. I wouldn't want you to have to wait around for me."

"No problem. I can stay and help too. What time should I pick you up?"

"Lana is doing something. She won't tell me, but she's coming to get me. But if you wouldn't mind driving me home, that would be great."

"Happy to. Now if you decide you want to try out dogs for a bit, I'd be happy to let Hero and Bitsy stay over so you can see what you think. They won't bother the horses and are trained. I can already see that Hero likes you."

"He does. How can you tell?"

"I can tell."

"Can I pet him?" She stole a glance at Hero.

"He'll love you forever if you do."

Christie reached over and stroked the Shepherd's fur. "Hey Hero. You were our hero today. Thanks for letting us know about the snake." As she cooed the words, Hero's tail thumped on the cement floor.

"Okay, I'll take you up on your offer. That might be a good idea to give the dogs a try. Especially after the other night."

"Tom told me about that. Did you get a look at the person?"

Christie shook her head. "Unfortunately, no.

Plus, he was dressed all in black and it was dark outside. He even knew where the cameras had a blind spot. We'll be addressing that right after the gala."

"What makes you think it was a male?"

Christie stopped and thought back to the figure she'd seen. She'd only glimpsed the person's back, but Bryson was correct. It could have been a woman or a man.

"That's a good point. I really don't know. It's disappointing that we didn't get them on any camera feed."

"Which means they know the operation better than most. Sorry to say it Christie, but there's someone associated with Horse Haven who's doing this."

"I was afraid to say it out loud. I can't imagine who wants to cause problems for us. To be honest, after Gabe's accident and then the peanut butter, I thought they were focused on you."

"Were you worried about me?" He winked, and Christie lost her response.

"Anyway, with this latest thing, maybe

someone wants to shut down Horse Haven. But who would want to do such a thing?"

"From what I've heard from chatting with Lana, developers were pretty persistent about getting this property."

"Yes, that's true, but there's still plenty of other land. I don't think this would be an issue."

"Anyone else you can think of?"

"Well, there was another vet who boarded horses who didn't seem too keen on us starting up. I think he feared that we'd cut into his business. But we assured him we wouldn't. Plus, for horses he's treating that need longer care, we allow him to bring them here at no charge. We've been on great terms since." Christie took in a deep breath. "I've been wracking my brain to figure it out, but no one comes to mind at this point."

"Well, let me know if you need anything else. We should be finished tonight, so we'll be out of your hair. Also, I gave the quote for your steps to Alice. Pop says if I do it this weekend, I'll get to try some chocolate pie you make along with some brisket he's cooking, so Saturday works for me."

The smile lit up his face and, for the first time, Christie noticed a slight scar on his eyebrow, going up into his hairline.

"You don't want to work on the weekends. I couldn't impose. I'm sure you have other plans."

"Nope. Plus, if I can get a delicious meal out of the deal, even better. You have my number, right?"

She nodded. "Up in the office."

"That's the company number. Got your phone? I'll give you my personal number."

She pulled the phone from her pocket, and they exchanged numbers.

"Good." He looked at her. "Looking forward to Saturday and thanks for the gala invite." He touched his fingers to the cap he wore, and Christie felt Hero come up and nudge her hand.

"Bye, Hero. See you later." Hero dropped his nose and, in long strides, met up with Bryson before the pair disappeared around the door.

She made her way up to her office and informed Alice that Bryson would be sitting next to her at the table. "Can you add him to the table roster for me?"

"Sure. Here are some messages for you. You know who he kind of reminds me of?"

Christie shook her head.

"A young Indiana Jones."

"You mean, Harrison Ford?"

"Yes, but not totally. Some other actors too, but I can't think of who they are right now."

"That's okay. It doesn't matter." She walked through to her office, plopping down in the office chair. She pulled her phone from her pocket as her phone pinged with a text.

See you on Saturday at nine?

Christie searched for the quote he'd emailed her. It was less than she had expected. She texted back.

Sounds good.

She hit send.

Mary's Tacos?

Yes, please. I'll have coffee.

Great. Anything in particular?

I'll eat whatever you bring.

My kind of gal.

Christie stared at the message. It was only a turn of phrase. She set the mobile down and struggled to focus on her work. She picked up her phone and rang Lana. "Where are you? Up for a ride?"

"That would be good. I can get them to saddle up two of the horses here. See you in twenty?"

"Super. Be over then."

Christie finished her work and met Lana out by the stables. Two beautiful horses were saddled and waiting. They pawed at the ground, ready to get moving. Lana and Christie enjoyed the silence as they let the horses warm up before letting them break into runs. They found the water trough and dismounted before letting the horses drink.

"I'm concerned about this latest incident. Maybe we need to think harder about that insurance policy."

Lana held up her hands. "I already told Don that we would discuss it in March after the gala and we took care of all the stuff afterwards. I don't know why he continues to bother everyone about it. I didn't tell him no, just to wait."

"The issue is, if someone were to get hurt and sue, it could be a big problem."

"It's all good. I had Alice pull the policy and unless something drastic happens, we'll be fine for now."

Unless something drastic happens.

Christie shivered at the thought.

CHAPTER TWELVE

The coffee was brewing when Christie heard a knock on her front door. She answered it to find Bryson with a big smile on his face. "Good morning. Looks like we've got some pleasant weather for getting this going today."

"Come in. Coffee?"

"Sure, if you've got it ready. I'd take a cup. Shoot!"

"What's the matter?"

"I totally forgot the tacos. I guess I was in too much of a hurry—" He stopped, as he realized he was rambling. "My apologies. I hate saying I'll do something and then not following through."

"I'm exactly the same. But don't worry about it. It's fine. Though you still owe me tacos."

"Deal." He smiled.

Christie pulled down a mug decorated with wild horses rushing across it. She poured the dark brew into the cup, then turned to him. "Need any milk or sugar?"

"No. This is perfect. Like the cup. You been a horsewoman all your life?"

"Pretty much. We had horses when I was growing up, but I didn't have any while I was working away for so long. I missed it."

"They're a lot of work." He sipped the hot brew.

"Yes, but so worth it."

"Well, it looks like you made the right decision moving home. Plus, now you're surrounded with horses every day."

"Yes—"

He cocked his head. "Why does that sound like a 'yes, but' answer?"

"Is it that obvious?" She grinned. "How about we take the coffee out on the deck? I need to wake up a bit more and there's just enough nip in the air to do the job."

"Good by me." He set down his cup and walked over to where Christie's jacket hung on a hook. "Let me help. You'll still want this." He held the coat up as Christie pushed her arms into the sleeves. She turned and faced him.

"Thank you." She met his gaze.

"My pleasure." He took a deep breath and gathered up the cup, taking it in hand, before holding the door open for Christie to go first.

Outside the sun's rays had crept over the deck creating a nice warm pocket, though Christie was still happy to be wearing the jacket. She sat in one chair while Bryson sat in the other, his legs spread with his forearms resting on his thighs. "Ah, I could get used to this. You're blessed to have this land and this view."

"It's not my land. It's Pop's."

He took a sip of coffee. "Yes, but unless you have siblings, it will come to you. Do you have siblings?"

"Nope. Just me. My mom got ill when I was fairly young. They always said I was their miracle baby as they never thought they'd have a child. How about you?"

Two younger sisters and a younger brother. One lives in Florida, one here, and one in Colorado. I love visiting there. How about you?"

"Yes, I've been. But not ready to go back yet." She cupped her mug with her hands, the warmth radiating in her fingers.

"Uh oh, bad experience?"

"You could say so. I was trapped with a killer in a bed and breakfast while a blizzard was going on."

"Whoa. You'll have to tell me—"

Christie's phone beeped. "Oh, it's Pop. Morning."

"Is that Bryson fella with you?"

"Yes, why?"

"I just made some biscuits and gravy, scrambled eggs, and bacon. Y'all come on over."

Christie moaned inwardly. "But Pop, I don't know his schedule and he's going to be working on the steps."

Bryson interjected. "My schedule's free. If it involves food, I'm there."

Christie knew she was defeated. "Fine, we'll be there in a bit."

After rinsing out the cups, they made their way downstairs and started walking to Pop's, keeping up a steady train of conversation. When they arrived at Pop's house, Mutt and Jeff rushed off the porch to meet this new best friend. With tails thumping hard, they danced around him as he laughed at their antics. Crouching down, he gave each of them pets, "Ah, they're great. Wish they could meet Hero and Bitsy."

"I don't know." Christie replied.

"Trust me, they'd get along great. My dogs look much scarier than they really are."

Pop came out on the porch, a dishtowel over his shoulder. "Quit 'cher dawdling. Food's getting cold."

"You heard the man." Bryson said.

"No dawdling." They said in unison, chuckles breaking out before Christie caught a glimpse of the smile on Pop's face. Ah, why hadn't she realized that Pop was trying to do some old-fashioned match-making? She gave him 'the look' but he shrugged like he didn't know what she was trying to convey.

Inside the food was piping hot, so Pop had to have seen Bryson arrive and given them just enough time before starting the food. It did hit the spot as Christie usually skipped breakfast. Pop regaled them with funny stories and the time flew by. After Pop waved them off, Christie and Bryson walked back to her house where Bryson pulled out an electrical toolbelt and put it on before grabbing some wire and a toolbox. He'd finished gathering the materials when his phone rang.

Christie glimpsed a slight clenching of his jaw before he answered the call. "Hi Becky. What's up?" He listened before responding, "Have you tried the breaker?"

He waited for her response.

"Okay, well, I'm on a job so I can't leave until later. If you can't get it fixed, call me and I can stop by tomorrow. No, that's the earliest I can come. Sorry."

He turned away from Christie as he listened to Becky, finally ending the call with a simple, "Okay, bye."

He faced Christie. "Now then, I'll get started on this. Can you show me where your electrical panel is located?"

After Christie led him to the panel, she went upstairs but she kept being drawn to the window like a moth to a flame, as she watched him working to affix lighting on the steps. Her phone saved her from herself as it was Orchid.

"Hi, Orchid. How are you?"

"Doing well. Listen I need you to stop by so I can see if I need to make any changes to the dress. Are you available today, say later this afternoon?"

"Yes, I can do that."

"I don't suppose you have any pie handy. I'm having a few friends over tonight and your pies are always a hit."

"What kind?"

"You pick. Gotta go for now."

"You too."

Hmm, what kind of pie to make? She'd made the chocolate pies for everyone to try out tomorrow. She turned on the music to an oldies station. Looking through her pantry she spied a bag of coconut. That was it—coconut cream pie. Christie set to work rolling out the dough for the pie shells. Her hands were covered with flour and dough when a knock sounded on the front door.

"Mind if I borrow your bathroom or I can find a tree outside."

"Guys. Of course, I don't mind." She brushed her hand across her forehead to move a lock of hair that had fallen forward, leaving a streak of flour. "Sure, second door on the left."

When he returned, he pointed to the pie shells that were now ensconced in pie pans.

"Ooh, hope there's a piece of pie I can have."

She wiped her hands before drying them on the apron she wore. "This is for my friend, Orchid, but I have enough to do two pies."

"Great. Well, back to work." He closed the door behind him, and Christie felt a void where his presence had been. She gathered the ingredients for the pudding middle and soon was pouring it into the pans. Whipping the meringue high, she finished the pies with a dusting of coconut flakes before putting them in the oven.

While she'd been rolling out the dough, her mind kept returning to the documentary about the Monarchs migrating down to Mexico. That would be cool to see that in person sometime. If there really was a butterfly effect, imagine what changes could occur with so many of them.

Thankfully, she'd already showered and dressed before Bryson arrived, so she was able to get ready fairly quickly.

The timer went off and Christie pulled the pies from the oven. The peaks of the meringue towered high above the pie and were toasted lightly. She needed to let the one for Bryson cool, but she put the other one into the pie carrier she'd retrieved from her pantry.

Gathering her purse, she went outside where Bryson was kneeling on the stairs, a pencil tucked behind his ear. A drill sounded as he made the holes to attach the lighting to the posts. He spied her at the top of the steps.

"Oh, here. Let me get out of the way." He made his way to the bottom of the steps. As Christie joined him at the bottom, he pointed to the pie. "Looks good."

"Coconut cream."

He laid his hand over his heart and stumbled

back as if he'd been shot. "No. Not coconut cream."

"You don't like it?"

"Are you kidding? Coconut cream is my favorite pie!"

Of course, it is. "Don't worry, there's one on the counter upstairs for you. It's cooling right now but if I'm delayed, could you stick it inside the fridge for me?"

"Yes, but hurry back so we can enjoy a piece together."

"Um, okay. Well, if you need anything—"

"All good. You're going to be happy when I'm done with this."

She smiled and nodded but in her mind she didn't want him to finish. He walked over to the truck and opened the door for her. "Here, hand me the pie carrier until you get in." She swung up into the seat and as he handed her the carrier their hands brushed each other for a brief second.

Christie, get a grip. You're not a silly schoolgirl, she admonished herself. Plus, he and Becky might be involved. She'd been so long without a relationship that she was equating being friendly to flirting. She backed the truck out, returning Bryson's wave. Being friendly or flirting, she'd enjoy this time, for however short it lasted.

After Christie made it to Orchid's she was told to go into a room that Orchid used for sewing. In the middle of the room, a shapeless form was covered with a sheet. Nervousness grew as Christie waited for Orchid to unveil the dress. She wouldn't want to hurt Orchid's feelings for all the money in the world, but Orchid was not known for her quiet restraint when it came to clothing. Today she was dressed in polka dot pants of assorted colors, a striped top, and a bandanna around her head.

"Ready?"

Christie nodded. Orchid removed the cover to reveal a dress of white muslin. Christie's brow crinkled up. This looked like the piece Orchid had made for the fitting.

"Um."

Orchid took Christie's hand and moved her a

foot to the left. Behind the first mannequin was a second smaller one. Christie gasped. The dress was a deep ruby velvet. The bodice was tight with a flowing skirt. A darker satin belt accentuated the waist. Along the top it was piped with the satin and was complimented by a lace shrug that had been dyed to match the dress.

"It's stunning."

"I hope that means stunning in a good way." Orchid winked.

"Of course, it does. Orchid, it's the most beautiful thing I've ever seen. Sorry for my first impression. It was hidden behind the other dress so I couldn't see it."

I often use the one in the front, so the covering doesn't crease or wrinkle what I'm working on. Plus, I love seeing the conception and the result."

"You're right. Now that I'm standing over here, seeing them side by side is amazing. To think that came from that idea. You're amazing, Orchid." She leant over and hugged the woman, tears pricking at her eyes. "Thank you so much."

"You didn't have anything to worry about child. I'd never do anything that would have made you feel uncomfortable."

Christie swallowed. It felt like Orchid had read her mind, yet once again. "I know. I was nervous, that's all."

"Understandable. The gala's a big deal. That's why I wanted to do this. One last thing you'd need to worry about for the night. I can't help you with the boots but with your vast collection I figure you have that handled."

"Yes, I have the perfect pair to go with this."

"Lana said that you all were going to get ready at her house, so I'll deliver the dress over there along with a cape, so you don't have to worry about staying warm or wearing a regular coat."

"You're the best." Christie felt she should pay Orchid for all her work, but she'd quickly learned that her elderly friend didn't care about money. Nor did she need any.

"Oh, I forgot the pie." Christie dashed back out to the truck to retrieve the carrier before returning inside. "Hope everyone likes coconut."

"I know they will. Now, didn't you say that Bryson fella was working on your house? Best get back to him." She winked.

"Not you too. Let me guess. Lana."

Orchid made a sign of twisting a key by her lips.

"I don't need a man."

"Exactly. That's why it seems like he's the right one."

Orchid waved to a chair and Christie sat down. "What do you mean? You've lost me."

"There's no denying you're a strong, independent woman. That's attractive to a man. You don't need him for anything. That means if he's able to capture your heart, it's because you want him. Just for him. Not for what he can do for you, or bring to the table in money, in prestige, or in anything else. Few are so lucky as to find someone that is already complete or isn't missing something that needs healing."

"That sounds pretty profound."

"I don't know about that. Have you ever heard the saying, when the student is ready, the teacher will appear?"

"Yes. Which is why you came into my life!"

"It's true that we met in a way that may never have happened except due to other events. For whatever reason, events have brought this person into your life."

"If Lana has anything to say about it, it was due to her prayers."

Orchid shrugged. "Not for me to say. But I will say this. Christie, give love a chance. Don't block it."

Christie's chest knotted. Was that what she was doing?

Orchid stood, signifying the conversation was over and Christie also stood. After they'd said their goodbyes, Christie waved at Orchid before driving off.

But as she drove back to Comfort, words and thoughts fought for attention in her mind. She needed to get home and write down her thoughts because if it were true, she finally knew what happened to Gabe and everything that followed.

What was hidden would soon be revealed.

CHAPTER THIRTEEN

Finally, the day of the nonprofit's open house and gala had arrived. Christie had woken at the crack of dawn to join the staff and volunteers for donuts and to ensure that everything and everyone was ready for the busy day ahead.

Horse trailers had blocked the entrance to the main barn with the offices so the caterer and others could work without being disturbed. Julie had set up a catering tent for the day and Bob had called in a friend who'd brought in his truck bed grill and smoker. Tables had been set up and a portion of the proceeds would go back into paying for the day's event and anything left would go to the nonprofit to fund the equine therapy program.

As families piled out of their cars, they were met by volunteers staffing the check-in booth. Every family was given a bag that contained information about the nonprofit's work, a magnet with a picture of the horses on it, and apple slices to give the animals. Becky had brought some of her alpacas out to the area and had a table with some of her products, with all profit going to the nonprofit that day.

Curtis waved as a group of families boarded for the hayride, and a farrier worked on shoeing a horse, explaining to the enthralled crowd about the process. Carol, who had recovered from her incident and looked much better, smiled as she chatted with parents about the therapy program and how it'd really helped her daughter.

Everything seemed to be going off without a hitch. Maybe she had been worried for nothing.

A hand touched her arm, and she jumped.

Turning, she saw it was Bryson. "Oh, you scared me."

"Sorry. I wanted to see how you're doing. Looks like everything is going well."

"I'm fine. Why do you ask?"

"I thought you might be worried about another incident occurring today."

Christie sighed. "You got me. I have been concerned after everything else that's been going on."

"That's why I came over early. I did a walk-through with Hero and Bitsy and checked every place I could think of that might cause an issue. I just finished another sweep, and all looks good."

"Bryson, that's wonderful. That really allays my worries. How can I ever repay you?"

"How about dinner next week?"

"Dinner?"

"Yes. You know, like food at a restaurant. You know, like, food." He mimicked a Christmas movie scene which made Christie burst out laughing.

"I don't know. I've got a lot on my mind right now."

He crossed his arms. "You have so much on your mind that you can't say yes or no to a dinner invitation?"

Just then, Becky walked over. "Hello. Can you believe it? I've almost sold out, and it's barely started. I'm going to run home and grab some more." She latched on to Bryson's arm as the ugly monster of jealousy rose in Christie.

"Bryson, would you be a dear and help me load some boxes into my truck?"

"Sure. I think we're done for now. Right?"

Christie replied, "Yes. We're done." She watched as Bryson left with Becky. She didn't have time for this, especially today of all days.

Christie turned and made her way over to the main barn where the activity was in full force as decorations were placed on tables, tech people worked at setting up the stage for the band and the podium. Large screens were already in place on either side of the stage.

Besides the catering, Julie had taken charge of the decorating and large trees filled with white lights created a beautiful entry way and were dotted throughout the barn. At the front tables papers and pens were placed for bidding on the myriad items. She was admiring a large painting of a scene in Comfort when she heard the sound of beeping as a large truck backed up by the entrance. Christie made her way to the doorway to spy a beautiful bronze work of two horses. This would be one of the first things guests would see as they made their way into the barn for the gala. Everything was coming together beautifully. Alice appeared out of nowhere, her hands embracing a folder and a large bag with nametags for the tables.

Alice's squealed, "Isn't this exciting?"

"Yes. The items up for auction are amazing. Artwork, boarding for a year, trips, it's incredible. Alice, you are to be commended for all your work on this."

Alice blushed. "I just want to make sure everyone's happy, that's all. I had a lot of help."

"Yes, that's a good reminder to put something together for all that the staff and volunteers have done to make this work."

"I'll look at some ideas and dates and let you know."

"Great. I see Don over there. I need to go speak to him, but I'll catch up with you soon."

Christie made her way over to where Don stood, surveying the comings and goings. "I just hope we don't regret not getting that policy before this."

Not this again. "Don, we've said we'll look into it depending on how much we receive from the donations tonight. A few weeks is not going to matter."

"Are you serious? A few weeks ago, we had a man die on site here. It's only that his wife didn't sue us for everything that we could settle with the insurance company. Then we lucked out with Carol."

"Yes, plus we avoided another possible unpleasant incident. Did you know about the snake?"

Don startled. "Why do you ask?"

"I didn't know if you'd been told about it. That's all." Christie took a step back.

"Yes, it was lucky nothing happened." He checked his watch. "I'm leaving, but if you need anything before tonight, you can reach me on my cell." He strode off.

Christie shook her head. "So much for pleasantries."

As the morning wound down, Christie was able to head home to gather her things and make her way over to Lana's. The woman greeted her with a sparkling mimosa. "Come in. Come in. I figured we deserved a bit of time for glamming up for tonight's gala. You especially after all the work you've done. Come on, we're all set up in the bedroom."

Curious, Christie followed Lana to her large bedroom with a seating area, where two women stood waiting beside a massage chair and a cushioned chair with a large tub full of sudsy water sitting in front of it.

"What's all this?"

"I traded with Susan here for some vet care for her horse. She offered her beauty services, and I said we could use some help glamming up for the night. I've already taken my shower, so it's all yours. Then do you want a back and neck massage first or nails?"

"Massage." Christie replied.

The afternoon helped calm Christie's nerves about the upcoming evening. After her hair was styled in a beautiful up-do, she waited until Lana had finished dressing into an aqua gown with brown feathery trim at the three-quarter length sleeves. She'd paired the dress with brown boots decorated with aqua rhinestones. Coupled with boots to match, the look was simple, yet elegant. "Now your turn. Off you go. I can't wait to see you in your dress. Orchid wouldn't let me look at it before you put it on so I'm dying to see it." Lana left the room, closing the door softly behind her to join the two women in the living area where they had waited to see the final results.

Christie slipped into the dress and smiled with delight as the velvet moved against her skin. It fit her perfectly. She found the cape made with the velvet and looped the buttons to close it. She stared in Lana's full-length mirror. The hair, makeup, dress, everything was perfect. How had she been so lucky to have such great friends.

When she moved out to the living room, Lana gasped as she saw Christie. "Wow! You're a knock-out."

"Thanks to these ladies." She pointed toward the two women.

"We only worked with what you gave us and

enhanced your natural beauty." They came over to take a closer look at the dress.

"That's sweet of you to say." She turned to Lana. "Ready to be envious?"

"More than I already am?"

"Look!" Christie showed them the pockets in the dress and in the cape.

"I'm so jealous right now."

Lana's phone beeped. She glanced down at it. "Perfect timing. Our chariot has arrived. Ladies, I'll check in with you tomorrow. Thanks for everything."

Outside, a handsome man in a white Stetson, white tie and tails and starched jeans stood holding the door open for them next to a limousine.

Christie gasped, "What in the world?"

"When I told Bryson that we'd be going to the gala in my truck, he said he couldn't have that, and that he'd pick us up."

"But it's like ten minutes away from here."

"Don't be such a party pooper. I, for one, am going to enjoy my time being pampered like a princess." She accepted Bryson's hand to help her into the vehicle. He turned and faced Christie.

"You look lovely."

"Thank you. You look nice too."

"Ready?"

"As ready as I'll ever be." She stopped as she held out his hand. "Listen, about earlier—"

"Already forgotten." He helped her into the car before joining them.

As the car made its way onto the nonprofit rescue's road, large luminarias with horse and saddle cut-outs in them dotted the drive. Lighted trees created a magical entrance to the front where individuals who had volunteered to be valets for the evening waited to serve attendees arriving.

Inside, Julie was chatting with her crew. She spied Christie and Lana and rushed over to meet them. "Everything's set. We'll pass out drinks and hors d'oeuvres for early arrivals as they're viewing all the auction items. At seven fifteen we'll begin passing out the salads, next will be the main course. After the main course, we'll clear for the presentation. Desserts will already be on the tables. A sliver of chocolate pie, a pudding cup, and coated strawberries." Christie had said something about the chocolate pie when they'd been discussing food and Julie had decided to use that recipe in the menu. After getting approval from everyone on the pies she'd made, she had baked two more as auction items. They were now displayed in glass cake stands.

"Perfect." A noise caught her attention, and she glanced up to see the rest of the board making their way into the facility. Everyone chattered at once, but Christie noted that Becky had stayed back to talk to Bryson. The woman's long blonde hair had been caught up in a rhinestone barrette and she was wearing a figure-hugging emerald dress. Diamonds sparkled on her ears, around her neck and on her wrist. Christie hadn't even thought to bring jewelry, so had borrowed a pair of earrings from Lana. Alice appeared, chatting with Carol, the pair laughing and smiling.

Christie spoke, "Here's the most important person of the evening. Alice, you want to point us to our tables?" Alice opened her folder and ushered board members to their respective tables. Finally, she took Christie to her table, which set right to the stage as to go up and down the stairs easily. She looked at the horseshoe arrangement of each table, leaving the side facing the stage empty. This allowed for better viewing of all attendees, and no one had to sit with their back to the stage, and the table decorations to be out of the way of the guests. In the center sat envelopes with a gold-embossed horse on the front.

While Christie had thought that nametags were a bit of overkill, Alice had been persuasive in stating that everyone liked to see their name and had made each one into a work of art with her calligraphy skills. To top it off, she had put them in small gold frames that people could use on their desks or in other spots, constantly reminding them of that evening. Christie had to hand it to Alice, they made the tables look spectacular. Christie found her name and moved over to look at the next name.

Bryson Taylor.

Oh no, how had Alice made such a mistake? She knew that she'd be able to do another one, so she better find her. She spied Lana over at the other table. She waved Lana over. "Do you know where Alice went? I need her to fix this nametag."

"Which one?" Lana gestured at the table. "They look right to me."

"Bryson's."

Lana burst out laughing. "That's his name."

"What do you mean?"

"I mean, the family's last name is Taylor. His dad started the business years ago kind of as a side business and everyone would just say, call Bryson. So, he named it Bryson Electric. The Bryson you know is junior to the senior who retired some years back. You know I hadn't thought about that until now, but it sure lets you know He's got a sense of humor."

"Who does?"

"God. I mean, come on. Of all the last names this guy could have, it's the same one you have. I can just see it now. God saying, 'I know that one. She'd pitch a fit about changing her name, so we'll just make it easier.' This is hilarious."

"Why would I change my—oh."

Lana held up her pointer finger. "Lana's prayers-one. Christie's stubbornness-zero." She blew a kiss and floated off in a cloud of perfume and pride.

Christie sighed. It had to be a coincidence.

~

The evening progressed without any mishaps, and when Christie read off the winning bids and names, she knew they'd surpassed their goal for the evening. She mingled with the guests as the band struck up the first song of the night and guests took to the dance floor. At the door, she and Lana stood to thank guests for coming and their contributions to Horse Haven. They were then handed a bag of treats, compliments of Julie's catering.

"How about a dance?" Bryson had appeared next to her.

Christie responded. "I have to say goodnight to the guests."

"Go!" Lana waved.

Bob had appeared behind them. "I'll take it from here. Take some time to enjoy your success."

Christie beamed. "It has been a success, hasn't it?"

He nodded. "Plus, we haven't even counted the pledges in the envelopes. I'd say it was a resounding success. Now git. Go have fun! You've earned it."

Bryson slipped Christie's hand in his, leading her toward the dance floor just as the music stopped and another song started.

"Ah, perfect." The lead singer sang about true love and broken roads. Bryson smiled at Christie as he spun her into his arms.

"Enough," muttered Christie.

Bryson replied, "What? Sorry, didn't hear you."

"I'm not talking to you."

"Um, okay."

"Sorry. That sounded rude. I didn't mean it that way."

"No offense taken."

Christie looked up into Bryson's face and swallowed. She had fallen deeply and completely in love and, try as she might, she couldn't deny it. As she looked at him, the thought of him and Becky made her want to flee and cry. But he smiled at her, and she decided to forget everything but that moment between them. She laid her head on his chest, listening to the beating of his heart.

CHAPTER FOURTEEN

Christie hadn't arrived home until long after midnight, exhausted from the full day of work and an emotional roller-coaster. The sun was up when she heard hammering. In her state of grogginess between sleep and awake, she struggled to determine if a woodpecker had set out to drill a hole in one of her wood beams, or if it was something else. She blinked and listened.

Quiet.

Good. Maybe it had flown away. She was drifting back to sleep when the hammering started up again.

"Ahhh!" Christie threw off the covers, padding toward the front door in her nightshirt and leggings. She flung the door open, yelling, "Go away!"

"Sorry, I was trying to get this finished for you today."

Christie screamed and slammed the door

shut. Had he seen her? How stupid could she be? Of course, he'd seen her. She cracked the door open and stuck her head out. "I apologize. I thought you were a woodpecker."

He laughed. "I've been called some strange things in my time on this earth, but never that."

"Funny." She wiped the sleep from her eyes. "I'll be back soon."

"Take your time. I'll work on something else instead of hammering."

"Great." She closed the door and shuffled back to her room, where she flung herself back onto the bed, gathering up her pillow in her arms. Unfortunately, the damage was done and there wouldn't be any way she'd get back to sleep. She flipped on her back, staring at the ceiling.

Why hadn't he knocked on the door, or was he still upset about how they'd parted last night? After their dance, she'd run over to Bob to ask if he could drive her home. He was reluctant, but finally said yes. Though she noted that he and Amy were later to be found in a dark corner in an argument.

Thanking Bryson for being her guest, she told him that the board and staff would be going through the envelopes and there was no telling when they'd be done to not worry about taking her home. Bryson's face had been a study of changing emotions as he listened quietly to her dismissal of him. The worst was when she'd held out her hand to shake his goodnight.

Even the thought of last night's finale left Christie with a sense of remorse for how callous she'd been to him. Yet here he was on her doorstep the next morning. Though it could simply be that he was finishing a job that he'd started for her.

Finally, dragging herself out of bed, she padded into the kitchen and put on a pot of coffee before heading to the bathroom to take a quick shower to wipe the rest of the cobwebs away.

When she emerged, she dressed in a knitted top and a pair of jeans. If the weather held out, she'd tried to get in a ride. She poured coffee in two mugs and went to the front door where Bryson was attaching a light fixture into a bracket.

He looked up as the door opened.

"Coffee break?" She held out the cup.

"Why not." He stood and dusted off the knees of his jeans, following behind her into the house.

She moved over to the living room sofa and sat down, Bryson waiting a moment before deciding to join her. They sat in silence, the only sound, the ticking of the clock on the mantel.

Finally, Bryson swiveled to face her. "I'm going to be forward and come right out with it. Why haven't you ever married?"

"That's forward, all right. I could ask you the same question. But first, how old are you?"

"Thirty-seven. Thirty-eight in March."

"Okay, while that's not on death's door, it's still a ways beyond the standard dating and marriage route."

Bryson stared off into the distance before finally answering. "I can't have children. As you can imagine, that puts off some women who long to be mothers. But the fact is, God said I'd know when the right person came along for me."

Christie didn't like the way the conversation

was going and squirmed in her chair, not sure how to respond. She licked her lips but said nothing in response.

"You're that person, Christie." His voice was low and firm.

She shook her head vehemently. "No, I'm almost ten years older than you. I'm too set in my ways. I'm not the right kind of person to marry."

"You're wrong. You're exactly the right person for me. And I'm the right person for you. You're strong and capable. You don't need anyone—or so you think. But as sad as it is, Pop's not going to be around forever. Friends are good too, but they won't keep you warm on cold nights or listen to your doubts and fears or share your joys. We're both future-oriented in our thinking, we both enjoy the same things, and we're right for one another. I've never said that about anyone."

"Bryson, I agree, we tend to think a lot alike from some of our conversations. Nevertheless, marriage is a major commitment. I'm not ready to make that commitment and, to be honest, I'm not sure I ever will be."

"I love you."

The words hung in the air and tears sprung to Christie's eyes as she struggled with what to say, even though she knew she loved him, too. Thankfully, Bryson stopped her from answering.

"Don't say anything now. I know you need to think about it, you need to review the pros and cons of your list, but deep-down you know I'm right and I believe that you've been waiting for me too."

He stood and looked down at Christie, who struggled to make eye contact with him. "I love you and I want to marry you, Christie. I know God put us together, so however long it takes, I'll wait." He picked up her hand and kissed it with his lips. "I'll see myself out."

He went through the door, and Christie bent over, gulping air. She listened as she heard him gather up his tools, make his way down the stairs, and then she rose from her seat to look out the window and watched as his truck's taillights grew smaller in the distance.

Finally, she walked to her bedroom, where

she sat on the bed. Taking in a deep breath, she opened the drawer next to her bed, where she kept her journal. She flipped to a page in the back where a line had been drawn down the center. The pros side list was lengthy, while the cons side only bore one word.

Afraid.

~

Pacing back and forth, Christie stood in her office. After Bryson had left, she saddled Champ up and rode over to see Lana, who also looked like she'd just made her way out of bed.

"What is it Christie? You've got something on your mind. Spill it." Lana trudged over to make coffee, then faced Christie, her arms crossed over her chest.

"He, well, he, I'm not sure—"

"You're driving me crazy! What are you saying? In plain English, please."

"Bryson as much as proposed just now."

Lana jumped up and down like a young girl, giddy with learning something exciting. "Do I get to be your maid, or is it matron of honor? How does that work if you've been married, but are now a widow?"

"Stop!" Christie buried her head in her hands as she fought back the tears that refused to stay contained.

"Oh Hun. I'm sorry. I thought you liked Bryson."

"I do. I—"

"Say it. You'll feel better when you do." Lana tilted her head and took Christie's hand in her own.

"I love him. How can that be? We barely even have known each other for very long."

"Time doesn't matter. When your souls connect, you just know."

"I guess. Still, I don't know what to do about this."

"Okay, so he loves you. You love him. What am I missing?"

"I'm afraid. We don't even really know each other, and yet I feel like I've known him my entire life. Like we 'fit' together."

"It's not surprising that this is causing you concern. You've been on your own forever. Marriage is a big step. I know when I married I had fears too."

"And look where it got you." Christie's hand shot up to cover her mouth. "Oh, Lana. I'm so sorry. I can't believe I said that. Please forgive me."

Lana took a moment before replying. "Yes, I lost my husband in a horrible war. My children lost their father. But that's the thing about love. Yes, you may lose it but that love that you shared will sustain you forever." She sniffed and wiped a tear from her eye. "My only regret is that I didn't marry him sooner."

Christie wiped her eyes with a napkin sitting in a stand on the table. "I guess I have some thinking to do."

"You already know. You just have to move forward. Relationships are hard. But that's what makes life worth living. Parent, child. Friends. Lovers."

Christie bolted up from her chair. "Oh, my

gosh. I've got it. I know what happened."

"What are you talking about?"

"The butterfly effect."

Lana shook her head. "Now you've really lost me."

"Listen, is the board coming in on Tuesday to go over the gala reports?"

"Yes. Why?"

Christie shook her head. "I need to make absolutely sure I'm on the right track with this, but I think I am." She leant over and hugged Lana before rushing out, leaving the woman with a puzzled look on her face.

Riding Champ home, more pieces of the puzzle fell into place until everything was clear-cut and evident. After dismounting, she pulled the saddle and harness off Champ before giving him a good brush-down. The ride had invigorated her, and her mind pinged with ideas that seemed to have been there all along and were only waiting for that key to unlock them.

It was the first time that she'd longed for the weekend to be over so they could meet. Truth would no longer remain hidden.

CHAPTER FIFTEEN

Christie struggled to concentrate on the agenda even though it was exciting to hear they'd far surpassed their fundraising goals. The open house had netted them sixty-five thousand after they'd paid for the day's supplies. They'd also been able to increase their monthly donor list, so they considered the day's event a success.

Yet, it was the gala that had surpassed all expectations, bringing in a whopping eight hundred thousand dollars. They could pay off the rest of the debt on the new barn construction, leaving them debt free. Some designated funds would go to equine therapy for veterans suffering with post-traumatic stress and their families. Lana was especially excited to get that program up and running.

In addition, the anonymous donor who had purchased the bronze horse statue had gifted it to the organization so it would remain in the front.

Finally, the group took a break from the work of the morning, and Christie knew that the time had arrived. She steeled herself for the fall-out of what she was about to do and share, but it had to be done.

The door to the office opened, and Alice came in, looking around the room. "Alice, please join us. You can take my seat."

Alice sat down in the seat that Christie had vacated. She took in a deep breath as everyone stole glances with each other, trying to determine what was to come.

"First, I want to thank everyone for such a successful event. It wouldn't have been a success without everyone working hard." She took a deep breath. "And yet, sadly, we're going to have to say goodbye to some board members."

Chatter rose from the table as confusion and raised voices questioned what she'd revealed. Christie sought to regain the attention of the group. Lana brought the conversation to a halt with a loud whistle. "Go ahead, Christie. Everyone pay attention."

"Have you all heard of the butterfly effect?"

Some heads nodded, while others appeared to be pondering Christie's earlier statement.

"For those who don't know, it's the saying that when a butterfly flaps its wings, it can cause a ripple effect. You've seen that if you skip rocks on a pond. And that's what happened here. One event—Gabe's accident, set off a ripple effect that has touched every one of us in this room."

Bob spoke up. "What's this about, Christie?"

"Since you spoke first, let's start with you, Bob."

He folded his arms across his chest. "I have nothing to hide." He looked around the table.

"That's not being truthful, though, is it?"

He made a face as Christie continued. "In fact, isn't it true that you and Amy are on the verge of an affair, if not already in one?"

His eyes darted toward Amy, who sat back with a smug look on her face. "We're adults. We can do what we want."

"That's true. But Bob's married. And yet, you still pursued him." Christie turned to Bob, whose blustery manner had disappeared, leaving him the center of attention of everyone else at the table. His face had turned an embarrassing shade of red, and he pulled at his collar with his finger.

Christie's voice lowered, "I have to say that I'm extremely disappointed in you, Bob. You have a wife and kids."

He didn't respond but stared down into his lap before placing his head in his hands, moving it from side to side. A hush came over the room as everyone sought a place to put their attention away from Bob or Amy.

Christie cleared her throat and continued, "It all began with Gabe's accident. I went to check the video and a piece of the video had been erased. Later, I went back after the event occurred with the doctored cakes, but it had been erased as well. I had to think about it. First, why was the footage erased, and two, who had access to do it. That's when I realized you'd done it, Alice."

Alice cried out, "I'm sorry. I only wanted to-"

Christie laid a hand on the woman's shoulder. "Protect others. Isn't that right?"

Alice bowed her head and nodded, a sob escaping from her lips as she fought for control.

"The fact is that Amy is a good friend, and the video showed her and Bob. Their affair would come out and you didn't want that to happen. You don't agree with it, but you're still her friend. But it was your devotion to your other friend that caused you to erase the second video."

Someone handed a tissue to Alice, who nodded before stealing a quick glance to her friend.

Carol's eyes met Christie's, but there was a new sense of strength behind them. "I gather you already know what I did."

"Yes. I can't imagine the burden you deal with daily. I had noticed you losing weight, the nails bitten to the quick. You needed help, but financially, there was no way to get any. When Don started talking about insurance, an idea came to you. If you were to be injured, you could go after the insurance company for money. You dusted those chocolates with the peanut butter powder." Christie moved closer to Carol, who kept her gaze fixed on Christie.

Her voice was strong as she spoke. "I'm ashamed of myself. I overheard Don talking to the insurance company about a payout for Gabe and I thought, if we could have some extra money, it would help so much. It's so expensive, with a special needs child and other kids to support. My husband is working himself to the bone and they're talking about cutbacks. If we lose that overtime, I'm not sure what we'll do."

"But after it happened, you changed your mind. You couldn't go through with it. That's why you never filed and when you came back, you dove into planning and reaching out to donors." Christie finished for her.

"Yes, I realized how foolish I'd been. Even with that little amount, it caused a worse attack than I'd expected. What if Bryson or someone else had ingested it? I'd never forgive myself."

"You'd planned on it, which was why you had the epi-pen on you instead of upstairs in the office in your purse."

"Yes." Carol replied.

Don sat forward at the table. "That's horrible. You could have driven our insurance rates through the roof."

Christie faced Don. "Perfect segway. I wasn't sure why you kept insisting on more insurance. After the incident with the snake and the fishing line, I realized that you had been the person who'd set that up. How much of a finder's fee were you getting?"

"I don't have to answer that."

"You're right. You don't. But you were trying to get us to invest in more insurance so you could receive money from it. I think a resignation would be in order."

Bob stood up from his chair, shaking his fist at Don. "Why you—"

"You don't have any room to talk with your...girlfriend over there." He pointed to Amy, who bristled at being called out. "We all knew what was going on with your pretend animosity of each other, and your sneaking off every time we had a break. You make me sick."

"Well, the feelings mutual."

Christie had to gain control back. "Gentlemen, please. Sit back down. I'm not finished yet." Everyone glanced at Becky, who was the only board member that hadn't been addressed. Her face was flushed, her eyes darting around the room.

"We have to start at the catalyst for everything else that happened. That starts with you, Becky. You wanted to get closer to Bryson, but he wasn't interested. The more you tried, the further he retreated. The old saying is true that hell hath no fury like a scorned woman. So, you decided to teach him a lesson. If he could get hit in the pocketbook, all the better. The day of the meeting you saw Bryson's truck, but you didn't realize that he'd lent it to Gabe to use that morning. Gabe went up on the ladder and once up on the scaffold, all you could see was a man with a white shirt and jeans. You thought it was Bryson. You snuck off to the electrical panel and flipped the switch back on."

Becky sprung from her chair. "I didn't mean to kill anyone. I thought he'd just get a small shock. But it was enough that he stumbled backwards and fell off the ladder. I feel horrible, but there's nothing I could do about it."

"You could have told the truth about what happened." Lana finally joined in the conversation, having been quiet up to that point. "Maria deserves the truth about what happened to her husband."

"It doesn't matter. I take back what I said. You can't prove anything. I'm leaving." She shot up and out the door, her heels clicking on the steps downstairs. She'd made it to the front barn door when a male's voice commanded, "Advance."

Two German Shepherds came from the sides of the barn, teeth bared as they barked at Becky, who screamed in fear.

"That's for Gabe." Bryson called the dogs to his side. "I didn't know you hated me so much, Becky."

Her voice pleaded. "I don't hate you. I love you. Don't you understand? I was hurt. I didn't mean for anything to happen to you or to Gabe."

A sheriff's deputy appeared. "We heard

everything." He clapped handcuffs onto Becky's wrists and led her out to his waiting vehicle.

Bryson made his way over to the group. "I feel horrible. Poor Gabe died because of me."

"You're not to blame." Lana placed a hand on his arm.

Bob spoke. "I owe everyone an apology. I've been such a fool, and I've been found out. I should tender my resignation too." He turned to Amy. "It's over. I knew it was wrong, but I needed to feel...something. I have a lot of work to do to make it up to my wife and kids."

"What are you saying? Don't say that. Bob, wait!" She followed behind him as he strode over to his vehicle, shutting the door on her.

Lana spoke to Christie. "Do you think that Amy will give up or go after him to get even?"

"I don't know. But to be honest, he deserves whatever happens."

Carol and Alice sidled up to Christie and Lana.

Alice said. "I expect you want my resignation as well."

Christie shook her head. "You were trying to protect your friends. While you chose the wrong way to do it, I can't fault you for that."

"But I should have realized what had happened as I'd seen Becky by the electrical panel earlier. I just never put two and two together."

Carol spoke, "I let myself get into an unbelievably bad place. I realized I'd been given a second chance when I survived my own stupidity. You can have my resignation too."

"Yes, I'll like your resignation from the board because I'd like to hire you."

"What?"

"I want you to be the assistant director. You can work part-time and decide what hours work best for you. Your kids are getting older and as they grow, I'd like you to grow into taking over my position. You have the passion for this organization and your insights on the equine therapy come out when you speak to donors."

"Are you serious?"

"Yes. You knew that no one else on the board or staff had that allergy. You didn't realize that

Bryson had it too. That's why you grabbed the cake and ate it right away. You figured that everyone would stop eating and most wouldn't have touched the desserts yet."

"Yes, I was going to pretend to knock the items off the table, but it hit me so quick, I didn't have a chance. I'm lucky to be alive. I'll regret that for the rest of my life."

Christie placed her hand on Carol's shoulder. "You were at your breaking point. I'm just thankful nothing worse happened. But I'm serious about my offer. Think about it. Talk it over with your husband. It will give you some additional income and allow you some time to be involved in growing the nonprofit."

"I don't know what to say." Carol smiled. "After everything I've done, that you would even consider me is a miracle."

"Mistakes are when you choose a wrong direction but decide to get off the path that harms you or others. It's when you know it's wrong but keep going that there's a problem."

"Thank you, Christie. I won't let you down."

She hugged Christie.

"I know you won't. You two will be a dynamic pair." She grinned at them before they walked away, chatting excitedly.

"Where's Don?"

"He slunk out the back in all the mayhem. I doubt he'll show his face here again. That snake may not have been a rattler, but it could still have caused some havoc. And who knows what would have happened if someone had triggered his booby trap."

"I think you could possibly press charges against him. Does that count as insurance fraud or —"

"Something to think about later. For now, I think that's enough for today."

"What about Julie? Anything there?"

Christie nodded. "Oh yes. I forgot. Remember, she was here the day of Gabe's accident. No one had seen her, but she'd been looking at where to set up tables. She saw Bob and Amy too. I don't know if she planned on doing anything with the information or not." Christie spoke to Bryson, "Did you ever figure out where you knew her from?"

"Yes. Turns out she's the little sister—well, not so little anymore—of a friend I went to school with. She'd dyed her hair, but I asked her about him and sure enough, they were siblings."

"Oh, good. Nothing bad there at least." Lana laughed as her phone pinged with a message. She glanced at it. "I've got to head over to the barn. Good seeing you, Bryson."

Lana gave Christie a knowing smile before walking away, leaving Bryson and Christie standing alone.

"Listen—" they both said at once.

"You first." Christie replied.

Bryson shook his head. "Ladies first."

"I can't deny that I have feelings for you. The idea of marriage makes me want to saddle up and ride away forever. I'm just not ready."

"When will you be ready?"

"I don't know, and I need to be honest about it."

He smiled. "I appreciate that."

"But I wouldn't mind going out to eat as a first step."

"You mean, like, food."

"Yes, I can do food."

"Great. Ready now?" He crooked his arm.

"Yes, I'm ready."

AUTHOR'S NOTE

Thanks for reading!

I hope you enjoyed reading *Death Steals A Kiss*. Please leave a review at your favorite retailer, on BookBub or Goodreads so that others can know if this is the right book for them.

If you haven't read the other books in the *Taylor Texas Series*, here they are:

> Death Takes A Break
>
> Death Makes A Move
>
> Death Stakes A Claim
>
> Death Steals A Kiss

Other cozy mystery series:

> *Backyard Farming Series*
>
> > Chicken Culprit
> >
> > Cordial Killing
> >
> > Honey Homicide
> >
> > Christmas Capers

Potager Plot

Duck Disaster (2022)

Viviane's Adventures Mysteries

Hijinks in Ajijic

Deception in Devon

Subscribe to get the monthly newsletter that has discounts, freebies, giveaways, and much more. Plus, you'll be the first to know about a new cozy mystery series in the works!

Sign up here: www.vikkiwalton.com